异质的风景

——当代世界女性小说创作面面观

Unfamiliar Landscapes

Aspects of Contemporary Global Female Fiction Writing

张 磊 著

中国财富出版社

图书在版编目（CIP）数据

异质的风景：当代世界女性小说创作面面观/张磊著．—北京：中国财富出版社，2013.6

ISBN 978-7-5047-4949-9

Ⅰ．①异…　Ⅱ．①张…　Ⅲ．①女性—人物形象—小说创作—小说研究—世界—现代　Ⅳ．①I106.4

中国版本图书馆 CIP 数据核字（2013）第 236381 号

策划编辑	王宏琴	**责任印制**	何崇杭
责任编辑	戴海林　苏　娜	**责任校对**	梁　凡

出版发行　中国财富出版社

社　　址　北京市丰台区南四环西路 188 号 5 区 20 楼　　**邮政编码**　100070

电　　话　010-52227568（发行部）　　010-52227588 转 307（总编室）

　　　　　　010-68589540（读者服务部）　　010-52227588 转 305（质检部）

网　　址　http://www.cfpress.com.cn

经　　销　新华书店

印　　刷　北京京都六环印刷厂

书　　号　ISBN 978-7-5047-4949-9/I·0088

开　　本	880mm×1230mm　1/32	**版　　次**	2013 年 6 月第 1 版
印　　张	5.25	**印　　次**	2013 年 6 月第 1 次印刷
字　　数	151 千字	**定　　价**	25.00 元

序　言

在当今社会，以女性为主体书写的、内容关于女性、以女性诉求为目的的作品确实已经在全球范围内占据了愈来愈显著的位置。然而，在女性书写繁荣与活力的表象之下，父权叙事的主话语似乎仍然在起着作用，其有效性并不弱于从前。不少女性作家对自我与身份的意识仍然在很大程度上受限于男性设定的固定化分类，仍然小心翼翼地探索着那些被男性认为是足够脆弱、足够“女人”的领域。有时，女性们甚至故意表现出一副男性人格，心甘情愿地抛弃那个困难重重的自我发现之旅。

幸运的是，在世界范围内，还是有相当多的女性作家敢于摆脱各种传统的规约，苦苦寻求她们自己的、别种的言说与书写方式。在她们的叙事中，她们或激进地挑战男性设定的有关性、家庭、室内生活的种种规约，或彻底改变男性设置的叙事规范。

具体来讲，今天的许多亚洲女性作家常常把女性灵与肉的话题推向深处，检测它的极限与张力。譬如，在经典小说《透光的树》等作品中，日本作家高树信子毫不迟疑地将她笔下的男男女女置入一个道德考验的境地，以悖论的方式向读者揭示着性别身体与金钱那种诡异、却也令人信服的动态关系。在《如光线般脆弱》和其他短篇作品中，越南作家黎明闺在这个问题上走得更远，甚至将革命忠诚度与人性的激情这两个看似矛盾的力量并置在了一起，由此揭示了越南女性的无助与复苏。在《切除》和其他短篇小说中，以色列女作家萨扬·利伯莱特则另辟蹊径，将她的叙事想象力聚焦在大屠杀的后遗症对当今以色列人生活的影响，这使得她有别于大多数同辈的亚洲女作家。

在欧洲的文学界，同样有许多女性作家取得了引人注目的成绩。譬如，在《英国来客》和其他小说中，英国小说家安妮塔·布鲁克纳对传统的英国妇女对他人近乎病态的依赖行为作出了犀利的批评，号召女性们勇于塑造更加独立的自我。在《只想要一个》和其他短篇小说中，法国作家克莱尔·卡斯蒂蓉几乎是以激进而决绝的方式重塑了我们对于一个母亲或母亲角色应该为何的期待和想象，以古怪的方式反映了微妙、但却实实在在存在的现代父权主义对女性心理造成的扭曲。在《玛丽亚》和其他作品中，意大利的大师级作家达契亚·玛拉依妮一如既往地保持着她独有的政治观与性别观。她小说人物的那种毫不妥协的姿态，旁人无出其右。在《黑桃皇后》和其他小说中，俄罗斯作家柳德米拉·乌利茨卡娅成功地改造了俄罗斯传统的现实主义文风，深入到了后苏维埃时代家庭淫威下受害者矛盾心态的深处。在《男人之味》和其他小说中，克罗地亚记者、小说家斯拉芬卡·德拉库利奇着力于意识形态控制与其对人性思维方式、心智的微妙影响，更是大胆地在叙事中探讨性禁忌，反映了东欧人在经历多重创伤之后扭曲的心态。

广袤的美洲大陆同样为具有创新精神的女性作家提供了足够的畅游空间。在《打击》和其他脍炙人口的小说中，美国获奖小说家苏珊·米诺捕捉到了很多意味深长的细节，揭示了典型男性霸权思维中各种细微的自私心理。除了米诺之外，少数族裔作家，譬如阿拉伯裔美国作家阿丽亚·尤尼斯和华裔美国作家李翊云，也都通过她们各自杰出的创作，成功地让主流社会听到她们独特的声音，为美国文学的多样化作出了贡献。在《我一直打算告诉你的一些事》和其他故事中，加拿大短篇小说女王艾丽丝·门罗挖掘到了人类很多冲动激变中凸显的人性本质，尤其是作为控制他人手段的偷窥癖。在《星光时刻》和其他小说中，颇具传奇性的巴西作家克拉丽斯·利斯佩克托将小说与哲学微妙地融合在一起，并且让叙述者与人物展开具有创造性的互动，这些都在很大程度上震撼、感动、启发了全世界的读者。从不止一种意义上来讲，她都算得上是“女性书写”的代表了。在《处女的激情》和其他故事中，智利的作家、翻译家露西亚·格拉展现了自己独异的才华，从普通生活和普通人身上发掘出神奇的一面，形象地展示出了人性深处那些最真实、最原始的感情。

大洋洲的女性之声主要集中在两个最大的国家，即澳大利亚和新西兰。在《母亲/家》和其他反传统的小说文本中，澳大利亚学者、作家斯尼亚·冈诺对书写的主题与形式都做了自由、大胆的处理，将固定的房子变成了流动的、可以争夺的两性战争场域。在《水中的脸》和其他具有高度自传性的小说里，新西兰作家珍妮特·弗雷姆提供了一个具有高度信服力、高度现实性的疯癫病例记录，尤其是精神病院里专制的、非人性的、只会引发恐惧和控制的工作机制。

当代非洲同样也为它土生土长的文学天才们准备了肥沃的土壤。其中，尼日利亚女作家奇玛曼达·恩戈齐·阿迪奇埃和津巴布韦女作家伊旺·维拉可谓技压群芳。在《私人体验》和其他作品中，阿迪奇埃洞烛了很多深刻的人性主题，譬如战争、种族纷争等对于普通人的影响，以及不同人群之间神奇的和解。在《无名》和其他小说中，维拉运用近乎难以想象的诗意笔法，探索了各种禁忌问题，展示了这个深受战乱国家严峻的现实。

张磊

2013 年 5 月于北京家中

Preface

In contemporary society all around the world, writings by women, about women, for women indeed assume a more conspicuous position. However, beneath the surface of this splendour and vitality of female writing, the master patriarchal narrative discourse seems to be still working, no less effectively than before. Many women's consciousness of selfhood and identity is still largely confined to the pigeonholed categories fixed by men, still cautiously exploring those delicate, feminine spheres. Sometimes, they even deliberately take on a male's persona, willingly abandoning the difficult and demanding path for self-discovery.

Fortunately, all around the world, still quite a few women writers dare to shackle off all conventional regulations, and seek their own, alternative ways of speaking and writing. In their narratives, they either radically challenge the sexual, familial and domestic norms set by men, or completely alter the narrative conventions set by men.

Specifically speaking, many Asian women writers nowadays tend to push the subject of female body and spirit further, testing its limits and tensions. For instance, in her classic novel *Translucent Tree* and other works, Japanese writer Nobuko Takagi never hesitates to put her characters in a morally-testing situation, paradoxically telling readers about the strange and yet convincing dynamic of sexual body and money. In "Fragile as a Sunray" and other short stories, Vietnamese writer Le Minh Khue goes even further by juxtaposing revolutionary loyalty and human passion—two seemingly contradictory forces in life, thus revealing the helplessness and resilience of Vietnamese women. In "Excision" and other short stories, Israeli writer Savyon Liebrecht focuses her narrative imagination on the after-effects of the Jewish Holocaust on contemporary Israeli life, thus setting herself quite apart from her fellow Asian contemporaries.

In the European literary scene, women writers have also made impressive contributions. For instance, in *A Friend from England* and other novels, British novelist Anita Brookner lashes fiercer criticism against conservative English women for their morbid reliance on others, calling for a more independent-minded self among them. In "I Said One" and other short stories, French writer Claire Castillon almost radically and thoroughly re-shapes our expectations and imaginations of what a mother, or mother figure should be like, weirdly reflecting the twisted psychology due to the subtle and yet mistakable oppression of modern patriarchy. In "Maria" and other works, Italian maestro Dacia Maraini maintains her trademark stance on class and gender, offering an uncompromising gesture that is hardly beatable or comparable by her contemporaries. In "The Queen of Spades" and other stories, vintage Russian writer Ludmila Ulitskaya succeeds in renovating the so-called conventional Russian literary realism, and delves into the ambivalent psychology of the victim under domestic terror in the post-Soviet phase. In *The Taste of a Man* and other novels, Croatian journalist and novelist Slavenka Drakulić wrestles with the ideological control and its subtle influences on human minds and ways of thinking, as well as audacious, taboo-breaking sexuality, reflecting the twisted Eastern European psyche.

The vast American landscape equally provides more than suffi-

cient room for innovative female writers to roam. In "Blow" and other eloquent stories, award-winning novelist Susan Minot from the United States manages to capture telling details that expose the nuances and subtleties of the archetypal selfishness of a male mind. Besides Minot, minority writers, such as Arab American writer Alia Yunis and Chinese American writer Yiyun Li, also manage to make their voices heard in their respective masterpieces, contributing to a rich and healthy diversity. In "Something I've Been Meaning to Tell You" and other stories, Canadian writer Alice Munro manages to dig into the essence of personality in the vagaries of human impulses, especially voyeurism as a means of controlling others. In *The Hour of the Star* and other novels, the legendary Brazilian writer Clarice Lispector subtly blends fiction and philosophy, and makes a creative interplay of narrator and character, never failing to surprise, move and inspire readers worldwide. In more than one sense, she has already been widely considered as the epitome of "écriture féminine". In "The Virgin's Passion" and other stories, Chilean writer and translator Lucia Guerra displays a rare ability to conjure the magical side in the ordinary life and people, vividly showing all the true and primitive emotions hidden beneath the human skin.

Female voices from Oceania are mainly concentrated on the two largest countries, namely Australia and New Zealand. In "Mo (t) he (r) /H (t) ome (r)" and other largely unconventional stories, Australian academic and writer Sneja Gunew takes liberties with both the subject and form of writing itself, morphing the immobile house into a fluid and contestable site for gender wars. In *Faces in the Water* and other highly autobiographical novels, New Zealander Janet Frame offers a highly convincing and realistic documentary case study of madness in authoritarian mental hospitals with their inhuman mechanisms of inducing terrors and controls.

Last but not least, contemporary Africa is an equally fertile ground for its native literary talents. Among its numerous stars, Nigerian female writer Chimamanda Ngozi Adichie and late Zimbabwean novelist Yvonne Vera certainly steal a lot of light. In "A Private Experience" and her other works, Adichie shows a rare insight into the profound human themes touching upon wars, racial and ethnic conflicts, and their impacts on ordinary lives, as well as the magical reconciliations between different people. In *Without a Name* and other novels, Vera employs a hardly believable poetic style to explore various taboos, revealing much of the unpleasant and grim reality in this war-torn country.

ZHANG Lei
May 2013, Beijing

目 录

第一部分 当代亚洲女性之声
Part One Contemporary Female Voices from Asia

第二部分 当代欧洲女性之声
Part Two Contemporary Female Voices from Europe

第三部分 当代美洲女性之声
Part Three Contemporary Female Voices from America

第四部分 当代大洋洲女性之声
Part Four Contemporary Female Voices from Oceania

第五部分 当代非洲女性之声
Part Five Contemporary Female Voices from Africa

第一部分
当代亚洲女性之声

Part One
Contemporary Female Voices from Asia

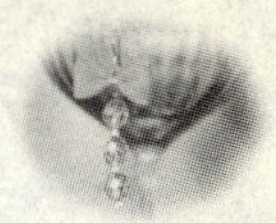

第一章 作为悖论场域与能指的性别身体与金钱

——读日本女作家高树信子的长篇小说《透光的树》

与当代许多女性小说一样，芥川奖得主高树信子（1946— ）的长篇小说《透光的树》也具有复杂的二元性特征——小说中两种对立、冲突的元素一方面不断地以各种方式彼此质疑、辩论，另一方面又交织在一起，无法分割开来。

如果仅看表面，这本小说在很大程度上就是一个平庸无奇的婚外恋故事。恋爱的双方都是中年人，分别是千桐和金井。具体来讲，他们在各自的情感压抑、空缺了多年之后，突然在彼此身上找到了强烈的共鸣和默契，然后又因为各种原因必然失去这份情愫，最后不得不在爱的记忆中疯狂地将其封存。

然而，在这看似太过规整情节的表面之下，有关这份激情的各种诡异的征兆开始显现，似乎在表明，这份激情并不能够被如此简化地理解，而是有不为人知的另一面。很多想当然的思路都不断遭受激烈的解构，这正是这部小说与众不同之处。

这个爱情故事的另一面主要与两个方面有关——一是作者对“肉欲”颇具模糊性的理解和处理。在小说中，它被主人公认定是一种高度可信的、真爱的形式；二是主人公对金钱古怪、但却也合情合理的共识，即它可以作为一种特殊的手段，使得被禁止或者不受祝福的激情变得正当、合理。

事实上有关性别身体或者说爱情的身体性这一问题，一直都被文学家们大力关注和探索，高树信子也不例外。在她看来，对肉体的“欲望”当然不是情感表达的一切。然而，它又确确实实在保持、发展男女关系方面起到了绝对性的作用。它绝对不是对真正爱情的否定或者是其对立面，绝对不是应该擦离或者掩盖于公众视觉之外的可耻行为。相反，它被抬到一个非常精神化的高度。这就是高树信子为何将大量笔墨用来描写千桐与金井之间的性爱本身，而且还调动了听觉、触觉、嗅觉、视觉等各种感官来强化这种美感。

吊诡的是，过于强化身体之爱的需要也具有致命性或者病理学方面的问题，因为它一旦走向偏执，便会无视一切他物，常常将情爱双方趋向非理智的边缘。性行为也沦为动物的本能，被疯狂、激烈地重复。性别身体被不知不觉地商业化了，变成了一种消费手段。有时，性行为甚至彻底变成施虐和受虐的实验。小说中那句看似非常哲学化的宣言（对笛卡尔“我思故我在”的激进式改写）——“我感故我在”(146)[①]，不仅令人感动，也令人心惧。不仅如此，一旦这种已经陷入痴迷状态的肉体因离开或者死亡的原因暂时或永恒性地“不在场”，就会对另一方产生毁灭性的影响，将其推进自我毁灭之路。事实上，在小说中，千桐在金井因癌症死去之后，确实因为他肉体永恒的“缺席”变得精神错乱。

小说中的另一个中心主题——性行为中金钱的模糊性地位使文本叙事进一步复杂化。对于主人公而言，这里金钱的指涉当然与传统意义上的内涵有所不同。通常来讲，人们很自然、也很正当地会把金钱看成是一种将性别身体物化，使其沦为卑贱、可憎地位的一种商业化手段。然而，在这部小说中，金钱悖论性地成为了一种积极的、好的手段，使得被禁止或者不被欢迎的激情（婚外恋）得以合法化、合理化。“不纯洁”的金钱反而变成了将“罪恶”爱情神化最“纯洁”的手段之一。从小说中可以看到，在千桐与金井之间以身体为依托的金钱交易中，从来就没有对交易规则或者条件作出任何清楚的规定，不论是金钱的性质（用于出

① 本章所引依据 Nobuco Takagi，*Translucent Tree*，translated by Deborah Iwabuchi（New York：Vertical，2008）．引文后括号内的数字为引文在原著中的页码。

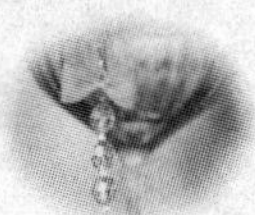

借还是购买性)，还是完成一次性行为应付的具体金额。如果我们不认真考虑这里的特别背景，很可能会把它解读为一种将金钱仅仅当做股子、投掷为乐的一种色情游戏。当然，这既不是商业行为，也不仅仅是个游戏。事实上，它同时暴露、又隐藏了主人公内心遭受了许久的恐惧和不安。对于千桐这个离婚许久的女人来说，她在精神上缺少必要的安全感，但是又对外在的世界与男性有着强烈的敏感之心。通过在她与金井发生性行为之中卷入金钱这一因素，她的内心可以实现一种奇怪的平静。其中，隐含的逻辑是，她可以努力（不管这努力到底结果如何）让自己去相信她自己真正需要的是金钱，而不是这个必然不断在变化着的、并不能保证永远可靠的男人。当她内心遵从了这个自我逻辑时，就可以更加理智地遵循自己内心的激情，而不至于被这种难得的激情之流盲目地将自己冲走，而是可以将其灌输到另一种激情当中。与此同时，既然未来不可预测，失去近乎成为必然，她倒可以自由地享用“此时此地”的这份激情，而不会觉得有任何内疚或者遗憾的心理。对于金井而言，他也为这种金钱行为找到了充分的合理性，因为它使他可以用自己的方式（一种实际、也是真爱的方式）帮助他爱的女人：既可以将她的父亲送到体面的医院，也可以改善她自己的生存状况。它也提供了一种自我欺骗的方式，来减轻他的自责感——尽管在自己家里感受不到任何爱的温暖，但他毕竟是个有妻子、有家庭的男人，很多责任是他不能、也不愿意摆脱的。

然而，一个行为的后果经常超出它的意图之外。在这个现代世界，金钱这个有意义的能指常常会具有高度的模糊性。它不仅仅“合法化”了千桐和金井之间的爱情，也不断地给他们的心理和心灵带来不安。即使对他们来说，这也绝对不是一个具有固定或者稳定所指的东西。相反，这一所指常常是多种多样的，具有强烈的任意性和流动性，逐渐地、必然地要摆脱他们看似牢靠的控制。譬如，尽管金井只是以钱为工具，并没有把他与千桐的关系真正看成是金钱关系，但他还是有了一种强迫性的心理：每次与千桐做爱之前都必须要先把钱给她，这必然会让千桐心生疑惧，误以为金井是在跟自己生气。与此同时，金井也对这种金钱行为愈加感觉不适，担心千桐最终会把金钱与她“作为娼妓的执照”(122) 错误地联系到一起。这是金井绝不希望千桐感受到的。然而，随着他们二人之间情与欲的发展，金钱确实微妙地改变了他们对彼此的理解和感受，至少给他们之间的关系设置了不少障碍，造成了他们经常性的忧郁、怀疑、误解，甚至是争吵。在“万能”的金钱面前，甚至是最理想化、最纯洁的激情也会被腐蚀掉，或者被部分毁掉。

情还是欲？物质还是精神？所有这些哲学化但又高度显著的问题自始至终都在伴随着小说的主人公。直到最后，这些问题也大部分并没有得以解决，因为不论是小说还是现实中，它们从终极意义上来讲就是不可解决的问题。但是，早已经神志不清的千桐的几句疯言疯语——“你这个右耳朵，是我的耳朵……你的右胸是我的右胸……”(188)，还有她女儿悄悄观察她母亲“衰颓的身体包含着巨大的幸福”(188)，都给这个充满失落与记忆的故事提供了某种“幸福的结局”，因为这说明在某些情形下，身体一面确实可以达到甚至超越精神一面。对于某些人来说，肉欲与任何其他事物一样神圣。

Chapter 1 Sexual Body and Money as Paradoxical Sites and Signifiers for True Love in Nobuko Takagi's *Translucent Tree* (Japan)

Alongside most of the contemporary Japanese fiction by women, Akutagawa Prize-winning novelist Nobuko Takagi (1946—)'s *Translucent Tree* features dualities that constantly question and debate with each other in many ways, and yet also inseparably get intertwined with each other.

On the surface, this novel is largely an all-too-common narrative of extramarital romance between two middle-aged people named Chigiri and Go, specifically their sudden and unmistakable mutual affinities after years of suppression, the inevitable loss of love, and the madly persistent memory of love.

However, beneath the all-too-neat surface, various signs of weirdness concerning this passion seem to show its other side that refuses to lend itself to a reductive interpretation. What is taken for granted is constantly subjected to vigorous deconstructions, thus setting this novel apart from others.

The other side of this romance mainly concerns two matters of consequence, namely the ambiguous understandings and treatment of "lust" as a credible form of true love, as well as the strange and yet arguable mutual consent on money as a special means of legitimatizing forbidden or unblessed passion.

The question of sexual body and the physical side of love never ceases to engage the imagination of inquisitive minds on the part of men of letters. Japanese writers including Nobuko Takagi are certainly no exception. In Takagi's understanding, "lust" for the flesh is certainly not everything. Yet, it does play a very decisive role in maintaining and developing the relationship between men and women, never being the negation to or opposite of true love. It is by no means a shameful act that has to be erased or veiled from public gazes. Instead, it is eulogized to a highly spiritual height. That's why Takagi spares no effort in providing an all-too-vivid portrayal of the way sex is consummated between Chigiri and Go, as well as the senses of hearing, touch, smell and sight that are strongly engaged.

However, to highlight the need of physical love can also be fatal or pathological, for it tends to drive the parties involved to the edge of reason and sanity when it reaches the state of obsession in sheer disregard of everything else. Sex becomes an animal instinct that has to be repeated relentlessly and fiercely. Sexual bodies are unwittingly commoditized as a means of consumption. Sometimes, sexual act is even sadistic and masochistic. The seemingly philosophical declaration (a radical rewriting of Descartean "I think, therefore I am") that "I feel, therefore I am"(146)① in the novel is not only moving, but also terrifying. Not only so, the loss or absence of the physical body in the form of temporary departure or eternal death can be so destructive as to push the remaining party to mental self-destruction in the end, as is testified by the deranged bereaved Chigiri after Go's death due to cancer.

Another haunting key theme that further complicates this narrative is the ambiguous role of money in a sexual act. For the main protagonists, money certainly means something different other

① Nobuco Takagi, *Translucent Tree*, translated by Deborah Iwabuchi (New York: Vertical, 2008). Subsequent citations to this work are given as parenthetical page references in the text.

than its conventional connotations, which often, and for the most time justifiably, regard it as a commodifying act that objectifies the sexual body, reducing it to a base, contemptible status. However, here, in *Translucent Tree*, money paradoxically serves as an active and good means of legitimatizing forbidden or unwelcome passion, namely extramarital affairs. The "impure" money turns into one of the most "purifying" ways to divinize the "sinful" love. As can be seen in the novel, in the financial transaction of body between Chigiri and Go, there is never any clear stipulation of any rules or terms, such as the nature of money (lending or paying), as well as specific payment for one specific sexual act (for example, how much should be paid for one spell of consummation). Without taking into serious consideration the specific context, this may be wrongly read as an erotic game in which money becomes a mere dice for throwing for sheer fun. Of course, this is neither a commercial act nor a mere game. It reveals and conceals at the same time the lasting fear and restlessness that constantly invade and torment the main characters' minds. For Chigiri, a long-divorced woman who lacks mental security and yet shows strong sensitivity to the outside world and men, involving money in their sexual acts can strangely put her mind at rest. The rationale is, she can teach herself, however futile the effort may be, to believe that what she really needs is money, instead of the ever-changing and unstable man. When she follows this self-fashioned logic, she can follow her passion with a certain reason and avoid being blindly overwhelmed by the flow of such rare passion and channelling it in another passion. At the same time, she can feel very free to enjoy the passion "here and now" without feeling guilty or regretful for its inevitable loss in the future. For Go, this money-giving act on his part can also be justified, for it enables him to aid the woman he loves in his way, a way that is as practical as truly loving, both putting her father in a decent hospital and bettering her own living conditions. It also provides a self-deceptive way to relieve his burden of guilt—although he feels unloved in his own home, he is still a man with wife and family, whose responsibilities he cannot and will not shirk away.

However, the consequence of an act never totally goes in line with its original intentions. As a meaningful signifier in the modern world, money can become highly ambiguous. It not only "legitimatizes" everything about the love between Chigiri and Go, but also constantly unsettles their minds and souls. Even for them, it is by no means a signifier with a fixed and stable signified. Instead, the signified tends to be multiple, arbitrary and fluid, gradually and yet inevitably getting out of their apparently firm control. For instance, in spite of the insignificant role Go casts for money in their relationship, he often has a compulsory need to give money to Chigiri before sex, thus necessarily arousing her fear that Go may be angry with her. Simultaneously, Go also feels more and more ill at ease for the fear that Chigiri may eventually make the wrong connection between money and her "license as a prostitute" (122). This is the least way Go expects Chigiri to feel. However, as they love and lust for each other, money does subtly morph their understandings of and feelings for each other, at least offering a few obstacles that contribute to their frequent melancholia, suspicions, misunderstandings, and even bickering. In face of the "all-mighty" money, even the most idealistic and pure passion can be eroded or partially damaged.

Love or lust? Material or spiritual? All these philosophical and yet highly visible questions dog the main characters throughout the narrative of *Translucent Tree*. In the end, they remain largely

unresolved, for they are irresolvable in the ultimate sense, both in fiction and reality. Yet, the already deranged old Chigiri's mad words "This right ear of yours, it's my ear... Your right breast is my right chest..." (188), as well as her daughter's silent observation of her mother that "the deteriorating body enclosed a vast happiness" (188) more than certainly offer a certain closure, a certain "happy ending" for this story of loss and memory, for the physical does equal, and even transcend the spiritual in some cases. For some, lust is as sacred as anything.

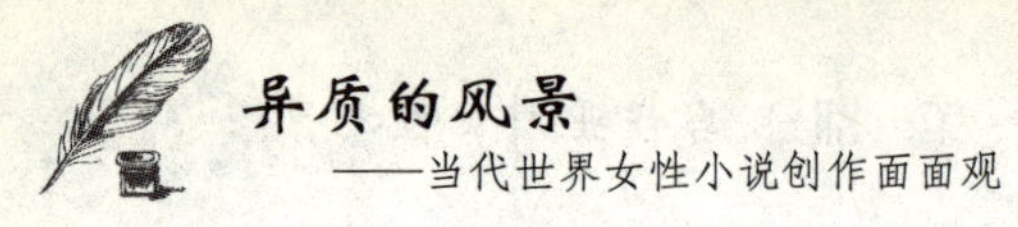

第二章　忠诚与激情的两难境遇

——读越南女作家黎明闺的短篇小说《如光线般脆弱》

作为当今越南首屈一指的作家之一，黎明闺（1949—　）在世界范围内都造成了较大的影响，这主要在于她在许多作品中深刻地反映了美越战争之前、之中、之后的越南生活。她从不直接、简单地探讨政治、战争以及它们对人的影响。相反，这些力量都成为她小说人物室内生活和回忆的有用背景或潜在因素。

在《如光线般脆弱》中，叙事者“我”向自己和读者都问了一个具有高度悬念性的问题：为什么他的母亲总是如此悲伤？他们在战后越南的社会地位、经济状况等方面都绝对算不上寒酸，没有什么让他们感到丢脸的。家里的孩子也都很听话，努力工作，在很多方面都很优秀。人到中年的母亲本人也仍然美丽、健康。在这样好的大背景之下，几乎没有人可以解释母亲为什么会经年累月地愁云密布，为什么还会偶尔发火，甚至哭泣。

这个悬念很快便被打破——叙事者接下来就开始对母亲战时的历史展开了巨细无遗的叙事。在那个时代，大写的“历史”被想当然地认为是要大于个人的、小写的“历史”。然而，年轻的女医生（叙事者的母亲）在战友们休息之后一次不经意的放松式散步，却让她突然看到了对面的俘虏。充满好奇心的她被这些特殊人群的存在深深吸引住了，其中一个人让她尤其动容，因为他的那张脸就是她想象中期待多年的一张脸。

根据战时的意识形态，尽管这种好奇心合乎人性，但还是已经放错了地方，因为它暗示着对未知的某种需要或欲望。对敌人有任何方面的兴趣都是不正确的，敌人就是敌人。

当俘虏与她的眼神交会时，这种好奇心就进一步被问题化了。可以说，这种眼神接触既是致命的，也是令人激动的，因为现在两人都不可避免地意识到了他们对彼此的兴趣，一切再也不可能继续被隐性化了。这种意识让他们都惊住了，不约而同地跳了起来，逃离于彼此的视线之外。

然而，这短暂的相遇还远未结束，俘虏发了高烧，需要医生治疗，几乎是命运安排一般，这个任务落到了女医生的肩上。

这次，两个敌人身份的男女终于有机会面对面地交谈了。在看他的时候，女医生的心中突然涌起了强烈的同情心，为他那双清澈、无邪的眼神，也为他那平静却又充满绝望的脸颊。只要是战争，就不可避免地具有残酷和非人性的特征，不会放过任何一个人，也不会让任何人毫发无损。当他告诉她自己之前的职业也是医生时，二人之间的吸引力似乎变得更强了。尤其令人震撼的是，俘虏此时对女医生近乎炽人般的凝视，让她避无可避——那是一种不是“出于恐惧……痛苦或乞怜”(67)[①] 的注视，而是“惊喜般的注视，因为在他一生中，竟然还可以发现一个本来可以属于自己的人，一个本来可以理解自己的人，一个本来可以与他共度一生的人”。(67)

在这一刻，这种凝视确实可以打碎一切。由战争而任意建构的敌我划分、对敌我双方激情或者爱情想当然的罪化，都遭到了彻底的解构。女医生和俘虏都在心里默默期待有朝一日可以重逢，并开始二人共同分享的新生活。

令人悲哀的是，现实总是很残酷，总是面目狰狞，逐渐将梦想与希望之光磨灭。二十年后，即使很多人为设置的藩篱都被拆除，他们仍然没有得以重逢，更别提共同分享什么新生活了。这里的希望确实如小说标题以诗意但也很悲剧化的方式暗示的那样:

---

① 本章所引依据 Le Minh Khue, *The Stars*, *The Earth*, *The River*, translated by Bac Hoai Tran and Dana Sachs (Willimantic: Curbstone Press, 1997). 引文后括号内的数字为引文在原著中的页码。

“如光线般脆弱”。这就是一个女人长恨之所在。悖论的是，正如叙事者略带调侃式的评论所说，这种未实现的欲望，倒也是一种新的希望，因为正是基于它的持续在场，这个女医生、这个母亲才能得以忍受惨淡的人生，坚持走到今天。毕竟，曾经的浪漫过往并不像看起来的那样毫无意义。

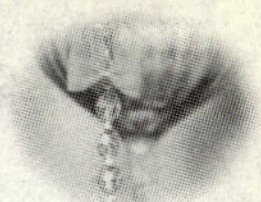

Chapter 2 The Dilemma of Loyalty and Passion in Le Minh Khue's "Fragile as a Sunray" (Vietnam)

As one of the leading Vietnamese writers nowadays, Le Minh Khue (1949—) impresses global readers with her profound revelations of the life in Vietnam before, during, and after the war with the U. S. in her numerous works. Politics, warfare, and their strong impact on humanity are never directly discussed. Instead, they often appear as useful backgrounds or in hidden strains in her characters' domestic life and reminiscences.

In "Fragile as a Sunray", the narrator "I" poses a highly suspenseful question to himself and the readers: why is his mother always so sad? Their social status and financial situation in post-war Vietnam, among other things, are by no means humble or humiliating. The children in the family are obedient, hardworking, and excellent in many ways. The mother herself is still beautiful and healthy in her middle age. It is practically out of question to account for the mother's gloom, occasional fury and cries.

The suspense is quickly dispelled when the narrator meticulously charts his mother's wartime history. During that time, it is taken for granted that "History" necessarily submerges individual histories or her-stories. However, the young female doctor (the narrator's mother)'s random roaming during her unit soldiers' sleep occasions a sudden sight of the prisoners on the other side. Out of mere curiosity, she feels greatly piqued by their presence, especially one with a face that has haunted her romantic imagination for a long time.

In wartime ideology, despite human nature, this kind of curiosity is already wrongly placed, for it certainly implies a certain need or desire for the unknown. It is simply not right to have any interest in enemies, who are supposed to be nothing but enemies.

This curiosity is further problematized when the prisoner's eyes meet hers. This eye-to-eye contact is both deadly and exciting, for they are both irrevocably aware of this mutual interest, which should have been left in the dark. Startled, they both jump up and run away from each other's sight.

However, this brief encounter is far from being over and done with. The prisoner's fever needs to be cured. As if by fate, this task falls on the woman doctor's shoulder.

This time, the two enemies finally have the chance to talk to each other face to face. A sudden compassion surges in the woman doctor's heart, for she sees all too clearly his clear and innocent eyes, as well as his peaceful and hopeless face. War, with its inevitable cruelty and inhumanity, leaves no one alone and intact. When he tells her his previous profession is also doctor, they seem to have even stronger affinities. What's especially striking is the prisoner's burning gaze that the woman doctor tries to avoid, though in vain, a gaze not "of fear... of pain or begging" (67)[①], but "a clear gaze of amazement that in his life he had discovered a person who could have belonged to him, who could have understood him, who could have spent his life with him." (67)

For the moment, this gaze is certainly all-shattering. The

---

① Le Minh Khue, *The Stars*, *The Earth*, *The River*, translated by Bac Hoai Tran and Dana Sachs (Willimantic: Curbstone Press, 1997). Subsequent citations to this work are given as parenthetical page references in the text.

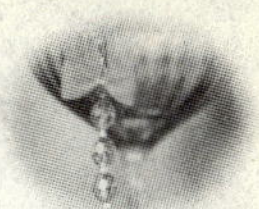

division arbitrarily made by war and the assumed illegitimacy of passion or love arising from so-called enemies are both subjected to vigorous deconstruction. Both the woman doctor and the prisoner secretly hope that one day they may see each other again and begin their shared life together.

Sadly, grim and cruel reality gradually erodes the glimmer of hope and dream, even after many barriers have been torn down. After twenty years, they still fail to meet each other again, not to mention having a shared life together. The hope here is indeed "as fragile as a sunray", poetically and tragically implied by the title. That's where the woman's eternal sorrows lie. Paradoxically, as the narrator wryly comments, this unfulfilled desire is also why this woman can endure her life until now. After all, a past romance is not that futile as it seems.

第三章 创伤记忆与强迫行为

——读以色列女作家萨扬·利伯莱特的短篇小说《切除》

多产作家萨扬·利伯莱特（1948— ）被美国著名女性主义作家格雷丝·佩莱热情地称赞为是她“以色列的姐妹”之一。确实，她以前所未有的强烈、而在情感上又颇为复杂的方式，成功地记述了当代以色列人的生活，以及它与犹太过去的关系。在她作品的多个主题中，一个经常会让读者无法不动容的主题就是大屠杀。当然，利伯莱特并未直接或者详细描述这一足以让任何人心生恐惧的行为，而是将自己的文学想象力集中于大屠杀对于幸存者残存的创伤性影响。

在《切除》中，利伯莱特一开始便描述了一件看似琐碎的小事——一位祖母给孙女剪头发。这位叫汉娅的祖母几乎是全情投入地做起了这件事，而孙女也很听话，脸上并未有什么不悦的表情。

剪发事件表面的琐碎性质很快便被解构——这位祖母工作时的表情很快被描述成“冷若冰霜，毫无表情，就像是着了魔的女人一般”(93)[①]。祖母的剪发行为愈发凸显出病态和令人恐惧的一面。当工作完成时，她“病态般激动地呼吸起来”(94)，她整个的身体也在“发抖”(94)。看起来，在剪完孙女的头发之后，她是再也没有丝毫力气了。她还告诉孙女，现在一切都会好的，她可以

---

① 本章所引依据 Savyon Liebrecht, *Apples from the Desert: Selected Stories*, translated by Marganit Weinberger-Rotman, Jeffrey M. Green, Barbara Harshav, Gilead Morahg, and Riva Rubin (New York: The Feminist Press, 1998). 引文后括号内的数字为引文在原著中的页码。

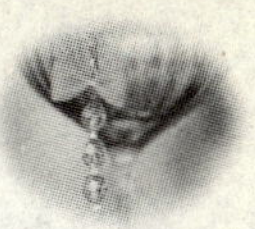

安心了。

然而，一切都不会再好了。当孩子摸到自己的光头，看到地上的碎发堆，情不自禁地恐慌起来，因为失去美丽的头发，她觉得自己变丑了，丑得像个男生。当孩子的父亲兹威克回家时，他也惊呆了，感觉自己就像是被重重地打了个耳光，甚至有一种垂泪的感觉。毕竟，他自己的孩子连自己都认不出来了。他情不自禁地怪罪自己的母亲，两次说她"疯了"(95)。

关于剪发，孩子的祖母当然有自己的理由。就像她之前跟孙女解释的那样，她跟她的儿子说，自己之所以坚持这么做，全是因为孩子的老师如此要求。是她要求所有的孩子一定要彻底把头发清理干净，以防头上长虱子。

对于兹威克来讲，这个解释很明显站不住脚，因为老师的这个要求只是一个善意的、而且经常会提的一个警告而已，每个孩子的衣领都会被别上这样的警告便条，根本就不能证明自己母亲这一极端、不理智行为的合理性。

从祖母的角度，她也不能明白为什么自己的儿子会把这样一个"严重无比"、生死攸关的事情看得如此无足轻重，因为虱子的危险几乎是大家都了解的公众信息，她的儿子知道，老师知道，任何看过这个警告便条的人都知道。

剪发事件在兹威克的妻子金娃回来之后达到了高潮。当她知道所发生的事情之后，立即勃然大怒，尖刻地批评自己的婆婆，认为她作出这一毫无理由的行为是愚不可及，疯癫无度，简直是犯罪。她一边无情地谩骂着，一边甚至要求丈夫将她一劳永逸地赶出家门，关到疯人院去，那里更适合她。

躲在儿子书房的汉娅无限伤感，静静地、也是无助地接受着儿媳对自己的种种指控。她情不自禁地想到了自己这种强迫行为真正、也是深藏的原因——毁灭一切的大屠杀对她产生的不可治愈的创伤。当她被关在奥斯维辛集中营时，有一天，睡在她旁边的狱友在睡梦中死去了。在这之后，她便有了神经质、精神分裂的毛病。她有了一种病态的恐惧，总觉得她死去狱友尸身上的虱子会离开她的身体，爬向另一个人的身体。这就是为何她不能容许这带着死亡气息的虱子爬到自己心爱孙女身上的原因。

不无讽刺的是，汉娅的这种逻辑除了她自己之外，没有人懂得。对于很多人来说，这一惨烈的过去应该被遗忘，被漂洗。他们拒绝让这一充满创伤的记忆继续损害他们的现在与未来。在某种程度上来说，这种集体的失忆是可以理解的。然而，它也同样具有潜在的破坏力，因为这种故意的遗忘使得以色列变成了无源、无根、无过去的存在。只有当今天的以色列能够以某种合适的方式来对待，甚至是欣赏汉娅的逻辑时，这个现代的犹太国家才能得到真正的重生。这是利伯莱特努力试图让我们明白的又一个同样重要的道理。

Chapter 3 Traumatic Memory and Compulsive Behaviour in Savyon Liebrecht's "Excision"(Israel)

Warmly praised by Grace Paley as one of her "Israeli sisters", the prolific writer Savyon Liebrecht (1948—) manages to chart contemporary Israeli life and its links with its Jewish past in unprecedentedly intense and emotionally complex ways. Among her many themes, one that often strikes readers is the Holocaust. Of course, the horror of this event is never described in a direct and detailed way. Instead, what preoccupies Liebrecht's literary imagination is the lingering traumatic effect of the Holocaust on its survivors.

In "Excision", Liebrecht starts by describing a seemingly trivial matter—a grandmother's cutting her granddaughter's hair. The grandmother Henya does it in an extremely whole-hearted manner, and the granddaughter is also very obedient, showing no unsavoury expression on her face.

The apparent triviality of this hair-cutting incident is soon deconstructed when the grandmother is described as someone who "worked with a frozen glaze, like a woman possessed." (93)[①] The grandmother's behaviour seems to be highly claustrophobic and scary.

---

① Savyon Liebrecht, *Apples from the Desert*: *Selected Stories*, translated by Marganit Weinberger-Rotman, Jeffrey M. Green, Barbara Harshav, Gilead Morahg, and Riva Rubin (New York: The Feminist Press, 1998). Subsequent citations to this work are given as parenthetical page references in the text.

When her work is done, she emits "a feverish breath"(94), and her whole body is "seized by a tremor"(94). She seems to be utterly exhausted by her work, and assures her granddaughter now everything will be fine.

But nothing seems to be fine any longer. When the child touches her clean head and sees the heap of hair on the ground, she cannot help feeling panicked, for the loss of her beautiful hair renders her ugly, and like a boy. When the father Zvic returns home, he is so shocked that he feels himself slapped hard and even on the verge of tears. His own child is hardly recognizable now. He cannot help accusing his own mother, calling her "out of… mind"(95) twice.

The grandmother certainly has her reasons for doing this. As she has already explained to her granddaughter, she tells her son that this is all because of the note from the child's teacher, who warns all the children that their hair must be thoroughly cleaned in case of head lice.

For Zvi, this explanation clearly holds no water, for it is nothing but a good and regularly done warning that is pinned to the collars of all the children, hardly justifying such an extreme and unreasonable act of making the child bald.

The grandmother can hardly understand why her son takes such a "grave", life-or-death matter so lightly, for the danger of head lice is almost public knowledge through and through, shared by her son, the teacher, and anyone who sees the note.

The hair-cutting incident reaches its climax when Ziva, Zvi's wife comes back. When she knows what has happened, she falls into a terrible rage, bitterly accusing her mother-in-law's stupidity, insanity and criminality for such a groundless act. In her relentless curses and swearing, she even demands the grandmother to be

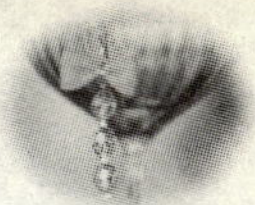

removed from the house once and for all, and put into a nuthouse where she is supposed to belong.

Infinitely sad in her son's study, Henya silently and helplessly accepts all the accusations pointed towards her. She cannot help thinking about the hidden and real cause for her compulsory behaviour—the incurable trauma left by the all-destructive Holocaust. One day, when she was imprisoned in the Auschwitz camps, her neighbour on the other side died in her sleep. She became paranoid and schizophrenic, for she developed a phobia that the lice would leave her neighbour's dead body and found their way toward another body. That's why she cannot allow the death-smelling lice to find their way into her dear granddaughter.

Ironically, this logic of Henya's is understood by no one but herself. For many others, this past should be bleached and forgotten. They refuse to let the traumatic memory continue to damage the present and the future. In a way, this collective loss of memory is understandable. Yet, it is potentially destructive, for it reduces Israel to a rootless being with no origin or past. Only when Henya's logic is properly handled and even appreciated, can the modern Jewish state and its citizens regain a real new birth. This is a further and no less important message Liebrecht attempts hard to drive home to us.

第二部分
当代欧洲女性之声

Part Two
Contemporary Female Voices from Europe

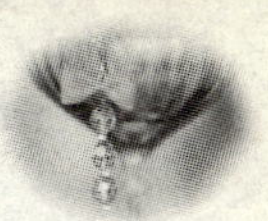

第四章 劝导与反劝导

——读英国女作家安妮塔·布鲁克纳的长篇小说《英国来客》

迄今为止，资深的英国作家安妮塔·布鲁克纳（1928— ）已经出版了二十四部小说，不论是在数量还是质量上都一如既往地保持着她不容小觑的水准。她的小说深入、专注地探讨了中产阶级男女（尤其是女性）边缘化的心理体验，以及她（他）们与周围世界、自我的矛盾性关系。有趣的是，虽然这些作品在主题上有相当程度的一致性，却并不显重复，几乎在每本新作中，都有喜人的创新与突破。尤其是她的第七部小说《英国来客》，显得尤为“异质”。

这一“异质”在很大程度上来自布鲁克纳对主人公即叙事者的选择。虽然她小说中并不乏人物形象身兼主人公与叙事者双重身份的情形，但是本书中的单身女性蕾切尔·肯尼迪仍然超出了大多数读者的意料。她在小说中并不是任何浪漫故事的主角，而是一个“观察者”、“评论者”。表面上看，她似乎在情爱问题上有着超然的客观和淡漠，颇有简·奥斯汀《劝导》里拉塞尔夫人、亨利·詹姆斯《使节》中同名形象的遗风。她主要关注的对象不是自身，而是他人——利文斯通家的女儿希瑟。因为全书基本上是第一人称叙事，所以她的视角不论“可靠”与否，都占据了很大的优势。然而，吊诡的是，这样看似老成、世故、“权威”的“劝导者”不仅最后在“劝导”一事上惨遭滑铁卢，甚至被“反劝导”了一把。当希瑟不温不火地讽刺蕾切尔之所以在情爱上失败、之所以试图劝说自己追求各种新鲜爱情，其原因就在于她自己的

“无能” (mismanagement)(198)[①]。这时，她一直精心构筑的单身世界的合理性、合法性便被残酷地“解构”开来。可以说，布鲁克纳从来没有在其他文本中让自己的女主人公面对他人——尤其是“学徒”如此深切、如此严肃的批评。

希瑟在结尾处的“反劝导”虽然让读者、蕾切尔都颇为错愕，不过却具有某种必然性、可预见性。首先，三十二岁的蕾切尔之所以被委以重任，看护一个仅仅比自己小几岁的小妹希瑟，在某种程度上便与她对希瑟父母某种“病态”的依附感有关。在父母去世后，她像是“孤儿”一般，失去了存在感。因此，她希望曾经为自己父亲做过会计的奥斯卡·利文斯通先生能够继续成为自己的朋友，并且希望自己可以成为“这样一个成功、不过也忧郁的家庭的一个有德行的成员”(13)。事实上，利文斯通一家甚至被蕾切尔近乎神化了，成为了这个不断变化世界中“固定的参照点”、“遵守着其他人都已经打破了的秩序”(31)。

从表面上来看，蕾切尔的这个愿望似乎确实实现了——利文斯通先生与太太多利·利文斯通似乎非常接受、欣赏自己，经常邀请她来自己的家，希望他们彼此之间经常保持联系。正是在这样看似“友好”的背景下，他们将自己的女儿希瑟“托付”给她，让她多给她提建议、出主意。

对于蕾切尔来说，希瑟并不是一个特别好“管教”或者规劝的女生，性格、价值观与自己可以说是完全迥异。不过，对自己价值观、单身观的自信（这在布鲁克纳的小说中非常特别），再加上希望维系友谊而需要付出的必要的责任感，还是让她接下了这个近乎不可能完成的任务。于是，她坚定地赋予了自己“猎场看守人”的角色。

这一角色虽然不像《钢琴教师》里埃里卡母亲那般变态、扭

---

① 本章所引依据 Anita Brooker, *A Friend From England* (New York: Vintage Books, 2005). 引文后括号内的数字为引文在原著中的页码。

曲，但是其超人的执着与坚定仍然令人侧目。譬如，当她第一次见到希瑟的未婚夫迈克尔·桑德伯格的时候，就有种不祥的感觉，几乎是立即就对他产生了怀疑："这样具有明显、不凡魅力的人一定是个骗子。"(42) 这种判断其实后来被证明是正确的——迈克尔确实不是个一般意义上的男人。他与希瑟婚礼上的着装便显得非常另类，不仅新娘一身白色，新郎也是故意穿上了一身类似的白色，很有"雌雄同体"的奇怪暗示。到了后来，蕾切尔更是偶然、但也是决定性地发现他在酒吧里涂脂抹粉、妖艳鬼魅的样子。

问题的关键不在于信息的准确与否，而在于信息的发出者对于信息的接收者到底有没有意义。换句话说，蕾切尔如此挖空心思、疯狂地想去讨好、关心利文斯通一家人，不仅让希瑟感觉"多管闲事"，也没有对利文斯通先生和太太产生任何作用——他们根本就没有把蕾切尔的话放在心上。正如利文斯通(Livingstone) 这个姓所暗示的那样，他们这家人从本质上来讲是排他的，他们的消极欲望如同坚石，蕾切尔对于他们来讲只是"英国来客"而已，根本不可能真正地同她亲密起来。事实上，不管希瑟如何一次次地让利文斯通夫妇失望，他们的心都永远只是向着自己的女儿。面对蕾切尔这个即使再好也是个外人的人，他们难以真正彻底地敞开心扉（不管他们怎么宣称如何需要她）。

事实上，早在希瑟与迈克尔举行婚礼之时，蕾切尔就已经隐隐感知到自己在利文斯通一家人心中并不算高的地位："我之前被认为是让希瑟得以提升的代理人，现在充其量只算得上是她荣光的反射器。"(49)

当希瑟与迈克尔离婚，很快与新男友马可去了威尼斯时，蕾切尔不得不"代理"女儿的责任。然而，她再次深切地感受到自己作为替身的地位："我感觉自己就像是某些关键性足球比赛的后备选手，虽然被认为是必要的，但却接受得有些遗憾。"(141)"本来应该在的是希瑟。"(142)

多利·利文斯通的卧病再次给了她新的考验。她像是圣经里的巡夜者一般，感受到强烈的死亡气息。然而，其他人对此毫无知觉。她自己也不得不收声，这近乎于她这样的人的“宿命”(165)。

希瑟的短暂回归给了蕾切尔再次“发声”的可能。她感受到希瑟在情感上近乎“流放”般的未来，希望再次感化她，试图说服她不要随便见到一个人便以身相许，要有必要的克制与谨慎。她甚至出人意料地“现身说法”，讲起了自己曾经的一次失败恋情，希望借以警戒她。

事实上，这时的她已经在逐渐失去自己一直以来试图建构的“说教”的权威视角，她试图论证的“理性说”本来只适用于他人，现在终于适用到了自己的身上。这些说教果然没有奏效，希瑟远未被说服，甚至被希瑟反唇相讥，“礼貌地”反问她：“就像你一样?”(156) 这让她感到了强烈的“无力感与羞辱感”(158)。

然而，吊诡的是，在多利·利文斯通死前，心中记挂的仍然是那个已经抛下自己、去威尼斯与新男友私奔、不争气的女儿。这使得蕾切尔决定要“继续把自己附属的角色扮演到底”(184)，出发去威尼斯，把希瑟带回来。

这样，蕾切尔又一次自愿踏上了注定要惨败的“劝导”之旅。当她终于在那里见到希瑟的时候，连希瑟的家门都不得而入，甚至当蕾切尔说她只需要跟马克称呼自己是个“英国来客”(202)时，都未能奏效。面对蕾切尔，希瑟能想到的，只是给她一个包裹，让她拿回英国。而且，她还近乎嘲笑地讽刺蕾切尔“总会为我们家做任何事”(202)，这也是她“最好的地方”(202)。言下之意，蕾切尔为了讨得别人的欢心，行为举止未免有些过于卑贱。蕾切尔之所以依附希瑟的父母，就是因为她“缺乏耐心和信心去为自己创造一种生活，总要依赖其他人的生活”(204)。不仅如此，她还让蕾切尔意识到自己选择独身的可怜、可悲，甚至只是个惹人“同情”(204) 的可怜角色。相比之下，不管希瑟的选择正确与否，却是“自成一格，要求自己的生活”(200)。原来，真正“陷

入危险的不是希瑟，而是自己”（203）。她彻底感到了“羞愧、缺乏，还有令人震惊的真相”（203）。

值得注意的是，为了更加深刻地阐释这个“劝导”与“反劝导”的主题，布鲁克纳还创造性地运用了“水”的隐喻，并且贯穿始终。

从一开始，蕾切尔便对水有一种莫名的恐惧。对于她而言，流动的水代表的是变化、不稳定。当然，水其实也是生命、活力的象征。因此，对于水，蕾切尔的态度是模糊、矛盾的。

希瑟和迈克尔结婚之后，选择去威尼斯度蜜月，这本身便暗示着他们即将投入到一种变化的生活之中。有趣的是，同事罗宾也在这时邀请蕾切尔去游泳，希望她克服对水的恐惧。在某种程度上，这不仅为蕾切尔后来的威尼斯之行做了一个很好的铺垫，更让她进入到了一种极度内省的状态。她开始把水与自己的思想对等在了一起——“对我而言，思想与悲伤的波浪相伴。”(62) 不仅如此，她还经常做一些有关自己溺水的噩梦。这些暗示都在告诫她，千万不要卷入到复杂的情感（不仅包括情爱，更包括任何亲密关系）生活之中。

然而，她没有意识到的是，从她一开始介入到利文斯通一家的生活时，便已经陷入了这种水一般的生活之中。她已经无法生活在生活的表面。当她最终去威尼斯试图唤回希瑟，被她羞辱之后，便感觉得到了这座水城处处的象征性含义，丝毫不逊于托马斯·曼的《威尼斯之死》：“我被水挡住了……又被水挡住了。”(203)

在某种意义上来讲，知识、即使是让人羞辱的知识，对于人的成长仍然是重要的。当蕾切尔在水城得到洗礼后，除了伤感和绝望，也获得了重要的自知，还有面对自己失败的力量。正如布鲁克纳本人所说：“这是个极为解放的年轻女性，大家不会再把她想象成是我的影子了！”

Chapter 4 Persuasion and Anti-Persuasion in Anita Brookner's *A Friend from England* (Britain)

So far, the vintage British writer Anita Brookner (1928—) has already written twenty four novels, all maintaining very high standards both in quality and quantity. Most of them deeply delve into the marginalized mentality of middle-class men and women, as well as their contradictory relationship with the outside world and their own selves. Interestingly, despite the consistency of subject, no single book leaves readers with the impression of repetition. In fact, all of them attempt to make innovative breakthroughs, especially her seventh book *A Friend from England*, which is markedly different from any other books.

This difference largely lies in Brookner's choice of the protagonist and narrator. In spite of the abundance of characters with such double roles, the single lady named Rachel Kennedy still exceeds most readers' expectations. In the novel, Rachel is not the heroine in any romantic relationship, but a silent observer and commentator. At a mere glance, she seems to be highly detached, objective and cold in loving matters, much like Lady Russell in Jane Austen's *Persuasion* and the ambassador in Henry James's *Ambassador*. What mainly concerns her is not herself, but someone else—Heather, the daughter of Livingstone family. Since the whole book is narrated in the first person narrator, her point of view certainly takes a very advantageous position in spite of its reliability. However, paradoxically, such a mature-looking, worldly and authoritative

persuader not only fails in persuading Heather, but also being persuaded. Heather spares no time to make a satire of Rachel, telling her that the reasons for her failures in loving matters and dissuading her to seek new love affairs lie in her own "mismanagement"(198)[①]. At this time, the reasonableness and legitimacy of her self-fashioned single world are relentlessly deconstructed. As it is, never has any one of Brookner's heroines received such blunt accusations and biting criticism from others, especially the younger ones.

In spite of the shocking effect on readers and Rachel, the "anti-persuasion" at the end of the novel on the part of Heather is indeed inevitable and predictable. First, thirty-two-year old Rachel is assigned such an important task as a chaperone for young Heather for no other reason than her morbid attachment to the Livingstones. After her parent's death, she feels orphaned, losing bearings in this world. Therefore, she hopes that Mr. Oscar Livingstone who used to be an accountant for her father, can continue to be her friend, and even hopes to become "such a virtuous member of just a successful but melancholy family"(13). In fact, the Livingstones are even mystified, becoming "fixed points of reference in a slipping universe, abiding by rules which everybody else had broken."(31)

On the surface, Rachel's wish seems to have come true—Both Oscar and Dorrie Livingstone seem to have accepted and appreciated her, often inviting her to come to their home and wishing to keep in regular contact with her. It is exactly within such seemingly friendly contexts that they decide to trust their daughter into Rachel's hands, hoping for more suggestions and advice from her.

---

① Anita Brooker, *A Friend From England* (New York: Vintage Books, 2005). Subsequent citations to this work are given as parenthetical page references in the text.

For Rachel, Heather is hardly someone easily disciplined or persuaded. In fact, they are a far cry from each other in both personality and values. However, Rachel's rare belief in her own values especially concerning singlehood, together with her sense of responsibility she feels to be necessary for maintaining good friendship with the Livingstone family, makes her accept this almost impossible mission as the "game keeper".

Of course, this "game keeper" is by no means mentally twisted or perverted like Erika's mother in Jelinek's *The Piano Teacher*. However, her extraordinary dedication and persistence in this task never fail to shock us. For instance, when she meets Michael Sandberg, Heather's Fiancée, for the first time, she has a strong sense of doom, almost immediately suspecting him: "a man of such obvious and exemplary charm must be a liar."(42) This judgment turns out to be right, for Michael is indeed no man in the conventional sense. Both his and Heather's wedding clothes look nothing but normal: the same whiteness that strangely implies androgyny. Later, Rachel accidentally, and yet decisively spots him wearing heavy powders and behaving suspiciously in bars.

The key point of a question lies not in the correctness of information, but in the meaningfulness of the sender to the recipient. In other words, when Rachel tries so hard to please the Livingstones, she achieves a highly ironic effect, not only making Heather feel that she is troublesome, but also failing to make any impression on Oscar and Dorrie, who does never take her words seriously. Just as the surname "Livingstone" implies, the Livingstones are fundamentally exclusive, who desire to remain passive, as if set in stone. For them, Rachel means nothing but "a friend from England", hardly being able to win their sincere familiarity. In fact, no matter how many times Heather fails to live up to the Livinstones' expectations, their

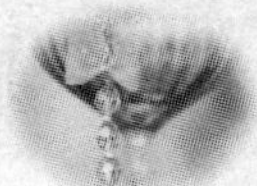

emotions always lean towards their daughter's side. Faced with Rachel, a girl who is ultimately an outsider, they can never really reveal their true hearts (despite their public claim to need her so much).

In fact, as early as Heather and Michael's wedding, Rachel has already sensed her unfavourable position in the Livingstones' hearts: "Formerly thought to be the agent of Heather's advancement, I was now to be the reflector of her glory."(49)

When Heather divorces with Michael, and soon goes to Venice with her new boyfriend Marco, Rachel has to substitute her as the daughter figure. However, she once again feels her lowly position: "I felt like the reserve in some key football match, accepted as a necessity, but with regret."(141) "I felt that Heather should have been there."(142)

Dorrie Livingstone's illness again brings her new tests. Like the watchman in the Bible, she feels a strong smell of death, which seems to be utterly unfelt by others. She herself has to keep silent. This amounts to being her "fate"(165).

Heather's brief return gives Rachel the possibility to make her voice heard again. Predicting a future of "exile" for Heather's emotions, she hopes to educate and move her again. She tries all means to persuade her not to devote herself too easily to others, and to hold enough caution and restraints. She even unexpectedly tells the lessons of her own love story to her, hoping for it to serve as an effective warning.

Actually, Rachel is gradually losing her moralistic authority that has been constructed for long. The theory of rationality no longer applies to others alone. This time, it finally falls on herself. Her moralizing not only fails to convince Heather, but suffers a counter-argument. In a deliberately polite-sounding way, Heather asks her: "Like you?"(156)

This makes her feel "exhausted and ashamed"(158).

However, before Dorrie Livingstone's death, what haunts her mind is still her wilful daughter who has abandoned her for her boyfriend in Venice. This leads to Rachel's decision to "play my subordinate part to the end"(184). That is, she will leave for Venice and bring Rachel back.

Once again, the almost stubborn Rachel sets on a fatal journey of persuasion. When she finally sees Heather, she can hardly find any way into her residence there. Even when Rachel tells her that she can be introduced to Marco as a mere "friend from England"(202), Heather is still untouched. Faced with Rachel, all she can think of is to give her a parcel to bring back to England. Besides, she greatly satirizes Rachel for her "do (ing) anything for our family"(202), which is "the nicest thing about you"(202). The implication is, to get other people's recognition, Rachel behaves in a way that is hard to be respected. The reason why Rachel has to cling to Heather's parents is that she "lacked the patience or the confidence to invent a life for myself, and would always be dependent on the lives of others"(204). Not only so, she also forces Rachel to realize her miserable and tragic state for choosing spinsterhood. Compared to Rachel, the impulsive Heather is someone who "strike (s) out and claim (s) (her) own life"(200), no matter whether she makes a right or wrong choice. After all, "(i)t was not Heather who was endangered, but myself. I felt shame, penury, and the shock of truth."(203)

Noticeably, to deepen the subject of "persuasion" and "anti-persuasion", Brookner manages to creatively use "water" as an important metaphor throughout the narrative.

From the very start, Rachel has an untold phobia for water. For

her, the flowing water represents change and instability. Of course, water is also a symbol of life and vitality. Therefore, Rachel holds an ambivalent attitude towards it.

When Heather and Michael marry, they choose to spend their honeymoon in Venice. This has already implied that they are going to be thrown into a constantly changing life. Interestingly, at this time, Rachel's colleague Robin also invites her to swim, hoping that she can conquer this fear. To some extent, this not only paves the way for Rachel's later visit to Venice, but also puts her into a highly meditative state. She begins to equate water and her thought—"Thinking, for me, is accompanied by a wave of sadness"(62). Not only so, she also dreams of herself being drowned. All these signs seem to serve as certain warnings for her not to be involved into complex emotions, including love and other types of intimacy.

However, what she fails to realize is, from the moment she gets herself involved into Livingstones' lives, she has already fallen into such water-like life. She can no longer live on the surface of life. When she finally goes to Venice for the purpose of calling Heather back, and is unexpectedly humiliated by her, she suddenly feels the symbolic meanings hidden everywhere in this city of water, reminding one of Thomas Mann's *Death in Venice*: "Iwas blocked by water… was again blocked by water."(203)

In a sense, knowledge, even including humiliating knowledge, still plays a very important role in a person's development. When Rachel is baptized in the city of water, besides sadness and despair, she also gets vital self-knowledge and the strength to face her own failure. In this aspect, even Brookner herself firmly believes Rachel to be a very liberated young woman, this time no longer fearing that readers may wrongly imagine her to be her own shadow.

第五章　激进地挑战室内空间

——读法国女作家克莱尔·卡斯蒂蓉的短篇小说《只想要一个》

可以说，当代很多的法国作家经常会创造出一套自己的关于小说如何来写的独特美学。这种独特性，或者更准确地说，创造性的古怪性，经常表现在他们敢于深入挖掘一些不寻常的、很少被人探讨的主题。巴黎新锐作家克莱尔·卡斯蒂蓉（1975—　）在这一探险的历程中当然也不例外。在她的很多作品中，总会有一股暗流隐藏在黑暗之处，反映着人与人之间扭曲、病态的关系。当这股力量扑面而来时，常常是在最意想不到的瞬间、最出乎意料的场景。

小说《只想要一个》一开头，卡斯蒂蓉便以她惯常的、略带邪味的方式，向读者展现了一幅虚幻的美景。一个男人爱上了一个女人，应许她未来的美好。他们有很多共同的爱好、兴趣，一起做很多事情，住的地方也足够体面，一切看起来都好得不能再好了。

然而，卡斯蒂蓉很快便以闪电般的速度揭开了令人不安的真相。事实上，发生的仅仅是一桩小事，但它却充分暴露了男人本质上的漠不关心。一天晚上，女人跟她的丈夫推心置腹，将自己内心终极的秘密告诉了他——她经常感觉到一个戴着面具的男人通过玻璃门进入他们的卧室。这种恐惧也许没有什么根据，但确实应该得到丈夫严肃的对待。然而，尽管他承诺一定会装百叶窗，却言而无信，把这事忘了个干干净净。

除了注意到男人的冷漠之外，女人其实心中还藏着另一层疑惧。表面上，她高调地宣称自己喜欢陪着出差的丈夫到处去旅行，

只有这样才能“让自己随叫随到”(8)[①]。然而，事实上，她这么做的真正理由是因为她有“自己的一套理论，知道男人独自出差时会干哪些勾当”(2)。这其实表明，女人从来就没有真正信任过男人对自己的忠诚和操守。他们不仅不关心彼此，也不信任彼此。

当男人要求女人为他生孩子时，对继续保持他们早已脆弱关系的最严峻挑战终于到来了。是他，而不是她要孩子。不过，尽管女人百般不乐意，千般不情愿，在“协商之后”(3)她还是屈服了。毕竟，她担心这个不靠谱的男人可能会“去别处得到他想要的”。(3)

但是，女人的这个妥协有一个条件，那就是她只能生一个孩子。因此，当她被通知自己已经怀了双胞胎时，她感到双重愤怒。一方面，她痛恨自己在抗拒多年之后还是走了和其他很多女人一样的路，沦为一个只会生孩子、养孩子的母亲。另一方面，她也担心双胞胎可能会在出生之时不正常。在精神高度狂乱、近乎歇斯底里的状态下，她向医生提议，希望他能够帮她打掉其中一个孩子。

尽管医生一再跟女人重申，她即将出世的双生子一定是健康的，女人对自己被强行分配的职责仍然非常不满。这种不满虽然暂时被压制，但却一直都没有消退。当双胞胎女儿出生之后，她经常会为她们的啼哭而备感心烦，甚至开始担心她们将来到青春期时会给自己带来各种麻烦。

女人被扭曲的意志最终得胜。一天，由于男人出差不在，所以女人不得不亲自驾车送两个孩子上学校。她们一如往昔地哭哭闹闹，让女人变得疯狂。当她发现车里的乘客座位根本坐不了两个孩子时，变得更加恼怒。最后，她干脆把一个孩子放在另一个孩子身上。她开车上路之后，孩子的尖叫声从来没有停歇，终于

---

① 本章所引依据 Claire Castillon, *My Mother Never Dies*, translated by Alison Anderson (Boston: Houghton Mifflin Harcourt, 2009). 引文后括号内的数字为引文在原著中的页码。

导致女人把车门打开，将坐在上面的那个孩子扔出了车外。

关于这一可怕事件的后果，女人基本上没有感觉到太多后悔，因为在她看来，她之前便答应男人自己只会生一个孩子，现在她做的并不违背自己对他、对自己的承诺。

从一方面来说，这个故事基本上就是由一个个令人震惊的心理、事件串联起来的，直接而又激进地挑战着室内空间的道德界限。毋庸置疑，女人在心理上是有问题的，至少是过于敏感了。然而，我们无法否认的是，无处不在的、无条件的、没完没了的男权主义确实在规约着女性的性、生育、家庭劳动，这其实是造成小说中这一可怕事件发生的、更应该被警惕、被注意的一个隐形原因。

Chapter 5 Radically Contesting the Domestic Space in Claire Castillon's "I Said One"(France)

Arguably, not a few contemporary French writers tend to develop a set of unique aesthetics in how to write fiction. The uniqueness, or more precisely eccentricity in a creative sense, often lies in the uncommon, seldom frequented themes they dare to explore, sometimes very deeply. Paris-based writer Claire Castillon (1975—) is certainly no exception in this adventurous quest. In her works, a clear strain of twisted and claustrophobic personal relationship invariably lurks in the dark, coming at you in largely unexpected moments and scenes.

In "I Said One", Castillon, in her usual wicked manner, starts by providing us with an illusory promise of good beginnings. A man falls in love with a woman, promising her a good life to come. They share many hobbies and interests, do a lot of things together, and live in a decent enough house. Everything seems more than fine.

However, Castillon never hesitates to unveil the unsettling truth at a flashing speed by narrating a small incident that fully shows the husband's inconsiderateness. One evening, the woman tells her ultimate fear to her husband that a masked man often enters their bedroom through the French doors. This fear may be groundless, but it should have been taken much more seriously. However, despite his promise to have shutters installed, he forgets everything about it.

Besides noticing the man's indifference, the woman harbours a more profound suspicion concerning her husband. Despite her high-sounding claim to love travelling from one place to another together with her husband on his business trips so as to "keep herself totally available for him" (8)[①], she does so largely because she has her "own theories about what a man gets up to do when he's alone on a business trip." (2) This amounts to saying that never has the woman really believed her man's fidelity and loyalty to her. Not only do they fail to care for each other, they also fail to trust each other.

The most challenging test for maintaining their already fragile relationship comes when the man demands a child from her. It is he, not she, who desires it. Despite the great unwillingness on the woman's part, she finally gives in "after some negotiating" (3). After all, she is afraid that he may "go somewhere else for what he wanted." (3)

The compromise, however, is made on one condition—she can only have no more than one child. That's why she feels doubly infuriated when she is informed of her being pregnant with twins. On the one hand, she hates herself following the same stereotyped path of being a mere child-bearing and child-caring mother that she has avoided and resisted for so long a time. On the other hand, she fears the twins may be abnormal during their birth. It is in this mental frenzy or hysteria that she suggests to the doctor that he can get rid of one of them for her.

In spite of the repeated assurance from the doctor about the physical normalcy of the expectant twins, the woman's hardly repressed dissatisfaction with her assigned role still persists in a dogged manner. When the two daughters are born, she feels very

① Claire Castillon, *My Mother Never Dies*, translated by Alison Anderson (Boston: Houghton Mifflin Harcourt, 2009). Subsequent citations to this work are given as parenthetical page references in the text.

irritated to hear their cries in their infancy, and even starts to worry about the upcoming troubles they may make in their teens.

The woman's twisted will finally triumphs. One day, in the man's absence for his business, the woman is compelled to take the children to school in a truck by herself. She becomes very mad to hear their usual cries, and even more infuriated to find no sitting space for the two of them. Finally, she just sits one on top of the other in the passenger's seat. As the truck runs on the road, the children's screaming never ceases, which finally drives the woman to open the car door and throw the one on top put onto the beltway.

Concerning the consequences of this horrible act, the woman feels largely unrepentant, for she used to promise to have only one child, and now she merely honours her promise to both the man and herself.

In a way, this story is indeed linked by one shock after another, explicitly and radically testing the moral boundaries of domestic space. Undoubtedly, the woman is psychologically problematic, at least hypersensitive. However, what should not be denied is that the pervasive, unconditional, and endless patriarchal demands on women in sex, reproduction, and house labour may well turn out to be a more hidden cause that should be greatly cautioned.

第六章　决绝的政治姿态与代价

——读意大利女作家达契亚·玛拉依妮的短篇小说《玛丽亚》

康皮耶罗文学奖获奖作家达契亚·玛拉依妮（1936—　）被广泛地评价为与意大利女权主义运动密切相关、最有影响力的作家之一。在她的作品中，她擅长描写各种局外人、边缘人的荒凉生活，尤其是那些在男性有意压迫下无法或者很难控制自己生活的受害女性的生活，不断地给读者以巨大的冲击。

在《玛丽亚》里，玛拉依妮成功地塑造出玛丽亚这个让人印象深刻的女主人公。在很多层面上，她都被剥夺了她本来应有的东西。然而，她却能在很多方面都能直接、高度意识到自己的现状，并以毫不妥协的方式加以反抗。

玛丽亚首先让人震惊的地方就在于她强烈的、毫不含糊的阶级意识。对于她的情人（叙事者“我”）还有其他工友来说，恶劣的工作环境与低工资确实让人很烦恼，但却也不是什么无法忍受的事情。在很大程度上，他们对自己的现状还是比较满意的，并没有觉得有必要、或者有太大必要去彼此交流，甚至是团结在一起去努力争取公正待遇。在玛丽亚看来，所有这些人都很可悲，因为他们这些被压迫者都已经被简化成非人的物体，已经变成压迫者的同谋。在政治良心方面，他们甚至“连动物都不如”(88)①。他们现在真正愿意做的，似乎仅仅是将自己彻底投入到日常琐事之中，想那些仅仅与他们自己直接相关的事情。

---

① 本章所引依据 *New Italian Women: A Collection of Short Fiction*, edited by Martha King（New York: Italica Press, 1989）. 引文后括号内的数字为引文在原著中的页码。

玛丽亚有别于其他人物的第二个特点是她公开的同性恋倾向。她拒绝把自己的这一行为仅仅看成是一时冲动。相反，她尝试着各种手段来为它的合法、合理存在找到正当的理由。事实上，她对酷儿身份的选择和她的阶级意识一样，也是基于强烈的政治动机。对她来讲，女性的生育能力只是被男人利用，以满足他们自私的、传宗接代的需要。在他们眼中，女人与生孩子的机器无异。因此，女性只有彼此相爱，才能摆脱父权的控制，才能成为真正的自我。尽管玛丽亚的这个逻辑仍值得推敲，但这一观点对于那些仍然固守霸权地位、拒绝给女人基本权利的男性沙文主义者来说，仍然是个沉重的打击。

有关玛丽亚的第三个显著特征是她对这个不友好、非人世界的终极反抗方式——自杀。由于她对自己作为农民身份的父亲在革命精神上的严重缺乏感到强烈不满，她很耻于与他们那些人为伍，甚至批判他们是愚蠢的自我主义者，除了钱什么都不想。与此同时，她的父亲也同样耻于她“不正常”(90)的性倾向，甚至让他的一个警察朋友把她关到精神病院去。对于他来讲，管她的女儿叫疯女人也强过管她叫女同性恋。对于玛丽亚这样一个具有反叛精神的女孩来说，即使被关进精神病院也不能够让她丧失斗志。相反，她继续号召里面的病人反抗。然而，这些病人似乎已经甘愿过这样行尸走肉般的生活，她的号召最终以失败告终。在幻灭与绝望中，她最终杀死了自己，来作为自己最后可能的反抗。

从一方面来说，玛丽亚的死是不可避免的。她无法妥协的政治雄心、期待让她无法容忍现状。然而，她这种强烈的、近乎顽固的革命热情在当下那个商业化、机械化的资本主义社会里又几乎不可能找到志同道合之人，甚至连她的同性恋女友、叙事者“我”都无法做到。不仅如此，她那种强烈的信念也必然会遭受到各种政治力量的规训与惩罚，甚至她的亲生父亲都做了她们的同谋。

总而言之，对一切既定权力者根本性的无法调和最终吞噬、淹没了像玛丽亚这样的无权者。她的生死形象地反映了那些无法适应现代社会的浪漫派革命者的悲剧命运，还有他们为了实现自己不屈理想而付出的沉重代价。

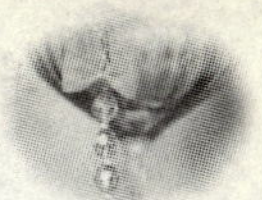

Chapter 6 Making a Politically Uncompromising Gesture and its Prices in Dacia Maraini's "Maria" (Italy)

Widely hailed as one of the most influential writers associated with the feminist movement in Italy, Premio Campiello-award winning novelist Dacia Maraini (1936—) never ceases to shock readers with her bleak portrayal of a variety of outsiders, especially women who have little or no control of their own life in their victimization by deliberate male oppression.

In "Maria", Maraini manages to create a highly memorable heroine in Maria, who is dispossessed in several senses, and yet explicitly and highly conscious of her condition and uncompromisingly rebellious on many fronts.

The first striking thing about Maria is her strong and yet unmistakeable class consciousness. For her lover, the narrator "I" and her fellow workers, the poor working conditions and low wages may be indeed annoying, yet they are still tolerable. They are largely happy with everything, and feel little or no need to communicate with each other and be united in their struggles for fair treatment. In Maria's view, all of them have already been sadly reduced to being mere objects and willing accomplices to their oppression and their oppressors. In their political conscience, they are even "worse than an animal" (88)[①], losing themselves in trivial everyday things and

① *New Italian Women: A Collection of Short Fiction*, edited by Martha King (New York: Italica Press, 1989).

thinking of nothing but what concerns them alone.

The second trait that sets Maria apart from other characters is her blatant homosexuality. She refuses to take it for mere impulse. Instead, she tries all means to rationalize and justify its existence. In fact, her choice as a queer is as strongly politically motivated as her sharp political consciousness. For her, women's reproductive powers are merely used or abused to meet men's selfish needs. Women are considered as nothing but machines. Therefore, women can free themselves from the patriarchal control and be their own selves only when they love each other. Notwithstanding the incoherence of its logic, this argument does strike a big blow to those male chauvinists who still cling to their hegemonic roles and deny women many of their essential rights.

The third noticeable thing surrounding Maria is her ultimate means to rebel against this hostile and inhuman world—suicide. Due to her ferocious dissatisfaction with her farmer father's lack of revolutionary spirits, she feels ashamed of him and others, accusing them of being stupid egoists who think of nothing but money. At the same time, her father is equally ashamed of her "abnormal" (90) sexual preference, and even goes so far as to ask his policeman friend to throw her into an asylum. For him, calling her daughter a mad woman is better than calling her a lesbian. For such a rebellious girl as Maria, even being put into such a place fails to dispirit her. Instead, she continues to call the patients there to arms. She hates their life like living corpses. In her final disillusionment and despair, she kills herself as the last possible protest.

In a way, Maria's death is inevitable. Her uncompromising political ambitions and expectations allow her no tolerance for the status quo. Yet, her strong and even stubborn revolutionary fervour can hardly find proper company in a largely commercialized and

mechanical capitalist society, even including her lesbian lover, the narrator "I". Not only so, her strong belief can even be disciplined and punished by political apparatus of various kinds, even including her own father as their accomplice.

In a word, this fundamental irreconcilableness with everything powerful finally devours and engulfs the powerless kind like Maria. Her life and death vividly mirror the tragic fate and heavy prices that those romantic and yet hardly adaptable revolutionaries have to pay for their unflinching dreams and aspirations.

第七章　家庭淫威下受害者的矛盾心态

——读俄罗斯女作家柳德米拉·乌利茨卡娅的短篇小说《黑桃皇后》

在当代俄罗斯文坛，享誉无数的俄罗斯布克奖得主柳德米拉·乌利茨卡娅（1943—　）无疑是个令人震惊的存在。她和大多数在后苏联时期急于挖掘各种前卫，或者实验性文风（如魔幻现实主义）的同辈作家迥然不同，近乎顽固地选择了托尔斯泰、普希金、果戈里、契诃夫一派的传统现实主义风格，并将其加以创新，在他们对人性的关注方面加入独特的女性、当代色彩。她的作品都很复杂，经常是把几个人性故事编织在一起，经常把那些过着乏味生活的灰色小人物与历史事件结合起来。她的作品里常有几个互相联系的主题：对宗教、族裔容忍的需要；苏联文化中的知识分子问题；作为文学主题的日常生活；新的身体意象(性别身体、残疾身体，等等)。

在她著名的短篇小说《黑桃皇后》（很明显，这个标题不仅仅是对普希金有关人性虚妄的同名短篇小说的随意借用）中，乌利茨卡娅成功地塑造出了一个特别的“危险女人”，以及她对自己家人实施的、无所不在的、长达数代的家庭淫威。

在这个短篇小说中，最显著的关注点是母亲与女儿之间颇具压抑性，但却奇怪地可以被忍受的关系。从一开始，“危险女人”姆尔就像幽魂一般，似乎已经隐藏在暗处。她无所不在，没完没了地索取，加速了她的女儿安娜衰老的过程。外人几乎看不出她们两人在年龄上有任何差别。更加讽刺的是，一天安娜因为做了恶梦，所以早起了一会儿，这竟然成为她难得的福佑，因为她终于可以有两个小时的自由时间，可以暂时逃脱母亲那颐指气使的

各种要求。然而，即使是这么一个小小的“偷来”的自由也很快就没有了，因为姆尔就像是一个真正的鬼魂，或者是一个从来不睡觉的监狱狱卒一般，突然间就从哪里冒了出来，出现在厨房里，像往常一样吆喝着她做这做那，而且还处处挑剔。让安娜自己都有些惊讶的是，她在母亲近乎无理的要求、命令面前，竟然永远都那么顺从，那么听话，总是会自发性地对自己所谓的错误作出响应，不断地找理由，不断地道歉。不仅如此，姆尔还习惯性地在女儿面前近乎无耻地吹嘘自己曾经的艳史，以高度色情、形象的方式讲述自己与各种著名的男男女女之间发生的那些风流韵事。

很明显，在姆尔一生当中，有两个重要的关键词：一是欲望，二是权力，而且二者复杂地联系在一起。一方面，对性和其他方面无尽的需要为无聊、重复的“行尸走肉”式生活提供了一种另外的可能。姆尔无法离开欲望而活，她无法摆脱欲望而乐——“她真正的不幸就是她不再想要什么了。”(84)[①]当她老去的时候，连死亡对她造成的危险也不是肉身的病痛或消逝，而是她再也没有那么多欲望了。姆尔已经变成了一个受欲望操控的强迫性神经质患者。

这只近乎不可理喻的母老虎之所以有这些无法停止的饥饿，这些无法满足的欲望，确实有一个隐形的，但是却也不难发现的原因，那就是苏联集权主义时期对意识形态全面控制所造成的精神倒退、腐朽和空虚，以及它对后苏联时期仍然残存的影响。就如安娜的前夫马里克曾经以半严肃、半开玩笑的方式评论的那样，“她（姆尔）和马克思列宁主义理论是一样，是永远不死的。”(86)安娜用同样讽刺的口吻，半同意、半否定地对他的评论做了回应：“他其实说错了。感谢老天，妈妈比什么活得都长。”(86)

从另一方面来说，姆尔生命中的“权力”问题也同样令人震惊。整个一生当中，姆尔都从来没有停止对权力的追逐，唯有如

---

① 本章所引依据 Ludmila Ulitskaya, *Sonechka: A Novella and Stories*, translated by Arch Tait (New York: Schocken Books, 2005). 引文后括号内的数字为引文在原著中的页码。

此才能摆脱无权无势的惨境。事实上，从一开始，她就明白，权力在一个专制、独裁的社会里意味着一切。作为女人，她感觉自己无力直接参与到男性争斗的场域。因此，她能做的便是用自己的女性魅力勾引一个又一个的权力者——不管他们是将军还是平民。唯有如此，他人才会意识到她也居于权力一方。她也颇具有变色龙的特性：不论谁掌权，她都会迅速地向其投怀送抱；每当这个相关的权力恋人失势，她也会以同样的速度离开他，另找靠山。很明显，在她对权力的追寻中，性成了供她操纵的、有效的、不可或缺的手段。

这种公共国家构建的意识形态甚至渗透到家庭生活之中。当姆尔人老色衰，再也无法通过色相来引诱权力者时，她便把自己永不枯竭的能量转向了自己的家，把同样具有压迫性的权力结构在家庭领域如法复制。她必须要成为这个家里的“黑桃皇后”。她的女儿、她的外孙女、还有她的重外孙子、重外孙女都变成了她统治下的奴隶。没人敢离开她，连一分一秒都不可以。那些哪怕稍稍表现出一点反抗的人，不论是安娜的丈夫、卡佳的丈夫，还是姆尔前任丈夫的全家，都统统消失得无影无踪，早就被遗忘，就好像他们从来没有存在过一样。

有趣的是，当姆尔的权力和欲望看起来要永远掌控每个人的生活之时，转折点出现了——安娜的前夫、一个已经在南非定居的波兰裔犹太人，突然给家里打了一个电话。他打算要回来看看安娜和自己的女儿。一时间，家里面长期男性缺席的状况便显得不尽合理、不合时宜了。安娜、她的女儿还有外孙开始有了质疑现状的意识。

尽管姆尔强力反对，安娜的丈夫马里克还是杀回了这个俄罗斯围城。他带来了很多新鲜事物，这些都是在俄罗斯很难看到的。更重要的是，他带回来了一种全新的精神，一种看事物、看周围世界的全新方法。甚至姆尔也感到无力阻挡他的影响。尽管她对马里克口诛无数，这位来客却似乎毫不被影响，甚至觉得这一行为颇有喜感，因为他只是把这个老太太当作需要迁就的病人罢了。

从“皇后”到“病人”，姆尔的地位确实发生了戏剧性的变化。这是高傲的她绝没想到的，尤其是在她根本没把他放在眼里的时候。

从某种意义上来说，马里克的回归确实具有强烈的象征性意义。这个被流放的局外人、这个“他者”，流放得确实好。他的财富、地位，还有新的精神状态都把姆尔这个老顽固彻底比了下去。当然，他这次回来并不是为了复仇，而是为了告诉姆尔和那些被集权主义扭曲的人，世界已经变了，不是变了一小部分，其他人(甚至包括姆尔）应该去尽情探索。她们应该离开这个牢笼一般的家，离开这个牢笼一般的俄罗斯，离开心的牢笼。

这一短暂的来访给安娜看起来安静，其实是绝望的生活带来了一丝希望，但是故事并未终止于此。在马里克回到南非之后，经常给安娜打电话，甚至邀请她、她的女儿还有外孙、外孙女来希腊游玩，以摆脱那个压抑的俄罗斯家庭。

这个秘密计划如果被母老虎姆尔知道了，一定会功亏一篑，让每个人都遭殃。这个死都不放权力的老女人一定会成为她们实现自己意图的顽固障碍。这一次，安娜这个长期受苦受难、但却从不抱怨一声的“圣人”(马里克语)，终于学会了在内心中默默反抗。她确实在精神上成长了。尽管她表面上对母亲禁止她们去任何别处的命令言听计从，事实上早已经坚定地作出了另外的决定，这也是她生命中第一次作出这样的决定:“不，亲爱的母亲。这次不行了!‘不’这个字虽然没有说出来，但是已经存在了。它已经被映射了出来，虽然不够引人注目，但却已经穿透靶心。她决定要直面她的母亲，不做任何前期讨论，便将一家人集体悖逆她的事实告诉给她听。”(106，107)

说“不”看似容易，其实要在内心里作出这个决定绝不容易。对于一个长期习惯外在集权制度和内在暴君对自己施行淫威的女人而言，那种持久性的创伤和折磨不是一般人能够想象的。要劝服自己去以其他的方式去思考、去感受、去行为、去表现，确实要有很大的勇气。

最终逃离的时刻越来越近了。安娜情不自禁地想象自己的母

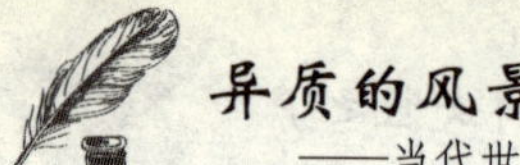

亲在发现大家离开之后会怎样的大发雷霆。只是，她现在再也不那么在乎了。回溯这段非常态母女关系的历史，现在的变化确实谈得上是激进得可以了：四十年前，安娜曾经有用家具打姆尔头的冲动；三十年前，她弱化到只有揪姆尔头发的想法。不过，慢慢地，她就什么想法都没有了。这些隐性的暴力冲动都在很大程度上被压制下去了，母亲的疾言恶语都慢慢变得习惯了。现在，在她离开之前，她终于又重拾了之前那种冲动，想要对自己因为这个老女人在场而深受的痛苦和磨难好好反抗一下，好好拿出点颜色看看——“突然，她看到，就像是一切已然发生一样，她自己、也就是安娜，把手在空中长长地摆动了一下，然而在那个涂满口红的老脸上结结实实地掴了一下，这一掴确实等得太久太久了”(108，109)。她感到了“自由和胜利的极好感觉”。(109)

然而，安娜还是做错了一件事，使得整个的大逃亡计划变成了一出悲剧。暴风雨将至，老太太似乎感觉到了什么，或者仅仅是像平常一样，疲惫地索要着——这次是要一瓶牛奶。倘若安娜拒绝跑到外面去给她买牛奶，一切就不会发生了。然而，安娜计算了一下时间，感觉自己做完这一切之后仍然来得及偷偷离开。就在她从商店买完牛奶回来的时候，就在她为即将到来的胜利狂喜不已时，她被车撞倒了，甚至还没来得及反应，就倒在地上死去了。

安娜的死让充满希望的机会瞬间化为泡影。本来，这个时间应该是大家为惨剧哀悼的时候。然而，姆尔却似乎并不为所动。她继续索要一切，终于逼得卡佳忍无可忍，替母亲安娜打了那个迟来的耳光。这一情景被描述得非常具体、形象：“卡佳走向姆尔，把手在空中长长地摆动了一下，在这张苍老，但并未涂脂抹粉的脸颊上结结实实地打了一个久违的耳光。”(110)

从某种意义上来说，这个耳光确实来得非常及时，算得上是为安娜报了仇，毕竟她再也无法作出这一姿势了。一个外孙女为了自己的母亲向外祖母复仇，这听起来有些匪夷所思，但却是实实在在发生了，也是必然要发生的——她所在的社会已经出了严

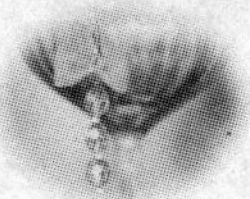

重问题，到处充满的是权力和欲望，而不是爱或人性。

姆尔在被打之后作出的回应让人备感震撼，因为她似乎由于这场悲剧有了一种病态的满足感和胜利感——她“安静但却清楚地说：‘看吧，看吧，到了最后，一切还是要听我的。’”(110)

听完姆尔说的话，卡佳作出的反应甚至让人更加沮丧。这个为了母亲狠掴自己外祖母的反抗型女人并没有带着孩子们去希腊旅行。相反，她“经过姆尔身边，来到厨房，打开纸盒，把牛奶倒进冰咖啡”(110)。这样的行为无异于宣告，之前所有逃脱这一牢笼的尝试均告失败。从终极的意义上来讲，他们根本无法逃脱权力结构的限制和控制。自由的意识虽在，但它还没有形成足够的力量，很容易就被打碎。对于那些早已习惯集权意识形态淫威的人来说，知道，行动，还要决绝地行动，必然要花更长的时间。

批评家海伦娜·葛熙罗认为，“尽管乍看起来，不论是女性中心主义还是打破禁忌，乌利茨卡娅的故事与彼得鲁舍夫斯卡娅的故事都颇为相似。然而，细细看来，乌利茨卡娅对道德行为的重要性与有效性有不可动摇的信仰，而彼得鲁舍夫斯卡娅却悲观地认为，人从根本上来讲就是在一个异化的世界里受到隔离和伤害。这种分歧使得她们有了很大不同。”然而，在乌利茨卡娅的《黑桃皇后》和其他很多小说里，我们还是可以清楚地发现深切的荒凉感和绝望感。这并不是要简单地否定葛熙罗的观点，而是希望强调两位作家本质上共有的叙事焦点——都是反映那些共有的、久久不绝的创伤与悲伤，这些感受在后苏联时期并未在俄罗斯人（尤其是俄罗斯女人）身上轻易地消除。乌利茨卡娅和彼得鲁舍夫斯卡娅写作的风格也许迥然不同，但是他们基本上写的是同一个剧本。

Chapter 7 Ambivalent Mentality of the Victim under Domestic Terror in Ludmila Ulitskaya's "The Queen of Spades"(Russia)

Arguably, acclaimed Russian Booker Prize winner Ludmila Ulitskaya (1943—) is a striking rarity in the contemporary Russian literary scene for her innovation of the so-called conventional Russian literary realism. Largely different from many of her peers who are all eager to explore various avant-garde or experimental styles (such as magical realism) in the post-Soviet era, she, almost in a stubborn manner, chooses to follow the traditions of Tolstoy, Pushkin, Gogol, and Chekov, and brings a unique female and contemporary hue to their humanistic concerns. Her works are complex, often weaving several human stories and layering historic events into the lives of gray, little people who lead a banal existence. A number of interlinked themes dominate her works: the need for religious and ethnic tolerance; the problem of the intelligentsia in Soviet culture; gender and family issues; everyday life as a literary subject; and new images of the body (the sexual body, handicapped body, etc.).

In her acclaimed short story entitled "The Queen of Spades" (obviously a more than cursory reference to Alexander Pushkin's same-name short story about human avarice), Ulitskaya manages to create a highly memorable character of "femme fatale" and the pervasive domestic terror she inflicts on her family members for several generations.

One of the most noticeable concerns in the short story is the

repressive and yet strangely bearable relationship between the mother and the daughter. From the beginning of the short story, the ghost of Mour, the senior femme fatale seems to be already lurking in the dark. In her dogged presence and endless demands, her daughter Anna seems to age unexpectedly faster. One can hardly tell their difference in age. More ironically, the early wakeup one morning from a bad dream amounts to a blessing for Anna, for she can finally enjoy one or two hours of freedom from her mother's domineering demands. Even this small "stolen" freedom proves to be short-lived, for Mour, as if she were a real ghost or a never-sleeping prison guard, comes out of nowhere and lands herself in the kitchen, starting her usual demands and keeping finding fault with everything. Even to her own surprise, Anna finds herself always so docile and obedient in front of her mother's largely ungrounded charges, for she never fails to spontaneously react, apologize, and try to find excuses for those things accused of being done wrong. Not only so, Mour also develops a habit of shamelessly boasting of her previous affairs with various famous men and women in a highly erotic and vivid way.

Obviously, in Mour's life, two key words, or motifs are highly conspicuous, namely desire and power, which are intricately interrelated. On the one hand, to make endless demands on sex and other things in life offers an alternative to the "living corpse" -like life full of boredom and repetition. Mour cannot live without desires, cannot be happy without them— "Her real misfortune was that she had ceased to want." (84)① In her old age, even the prospect for death is terrible for no other reason than that she will cease to want.

① Ludmila Ulitskaya, *Sonechka: A Novella and Stories*, translated by Arch Tait (New York: Schocken Books, 2005). Subsequent citations to this work are given as parenthetical page references in the text.

Mour becomes a compulsory neurotic for desire itself.

This unquenchable hunger, this insatiable desire on the part of this impossible tigress does have a hidden and yet not indiscernible cause: the spiritual degradation, depravity and emptiness in the ideology-controlling Soviet state and its lasting impact even after its demise. As the returned Marek, ex-husband of Anna, once commented in a half-joking, half-serious manner, "she was as deathless as the theory of Marxism-Lenism." (86) Anna, in an equally satirical tone, agrees and disagrees with this comment by saying, "he was wrong. Mama, thank heaven, has even outlived Marxism."(86)

On the other hand, the "power" motif in Mour's life is no less shocking. Throughout her life, Mour never ceases to chase after power so as to escape any possibility of powerlessness. In fact, from the very beginning, she knows power means everything in a dictatorial and authoritarian society. As a woman, she feels incapable of participating directly in the area of male struggle. As a result, she starts to bewitch and seduce one powerful man after another, generals or civilians, so as to make other people recognize herself as part of the power establishment. Whoever has power or position, she will give herself to him at a flashing speed. Whenever the lover concerned collapses, she will flee him at an equally flashing speed and find someone else for support. Noticeably, in her quest for power, sexual desires become an effective and indispensable means at her disposal.

The public, state-shaped ideology has even infiltrated itself into domesticity. When Mour finally gets too old to be someone useful in arousing men's lust, she shifts her inexhaustible energy for power back into her own home, and reproduces the same oppressive power structure within her domestic terrains. She has to be the "Queen of

Spades". His daughter, her granddaughter, and her grand-grand children become obidient slaves to her governance. No one can or dare get away from her, not for one minute. Those who show the least resistance, such as Anna's husband, Katya's husband, the entire family of Mour's last husband, all disappear and are forgotten as if they had never existed.

Interestingly, when Mour's power and desire seem to govern everyone's life eternally, a turning point presents itself—the unexpected call from Anna's ex-husband, a Polish Jew, who has already been well settled in South Africa. He intends to pay a visit to Anna and his daughter. The foundation for such a long absence of any redeeming force in the form of a man is suddenly made unjustifiable. Anna, her daughter and her grandchildren start to have the consciousness to question the status quo.

Despite the ferocious disagreement from Mour, Anna's husband Marek still makes his way back into the fortress besieged. He brings everything new, everything that is seldom seen in a poor country that is Russia. What's more important, he brings there a new spirit, a new way to look at things and the world around. Even Mour feels incapable of preventing his influences. Although she lashes various verbal attacks against Marek, the visitor seems unperturbed and even amused. He simply treats the old lady as one of his patients that need to be humored. From a "queen" to a "patient", Mour's status is indeed turned upside down. This is the least thing she expects from an intrusive visitor that she never takes seriously.

In a sense, the return of Marek is indeed highly symbolic. The exiled outsider, the "other", is exiled with a good result. His fortune, status and new mentality all put Mour in the shade. Of course, he is not back as an avenger, for he is more than an avenger. He returns to tell and show Mour and those damaged by totalitarian mentalities that the world has changed, not partially, but fundamentally. There is something outside for Anna and others, even including Mour, to discover and explore. They should be outside the prison-like house, outside the prison-like Russia, outside the prison house of the soul.

The brief visit sends a ripple of hope in Anna's seemingly peaceful and actually hopeless life, but it never simply ends there. After Marek returns to South Africa, he makes frequent calls to Anna, and eventually invites Anna, her daughter and grandchildren to Greece for relief from the suffocation of their Russian home.

If made known to the tigress, this plan is bound to be devastating, wreaking havoc on everyone at hand. The power-clinging old dowager is bound to become the diehard obstacle to their intentions. This time, Anna, the long-suffering and never complaining "saint" (in Marek's words), finally learns to rebel silently in her heart. She grows up in the spiritual sense. Despite her apparent obedience to her mother's roaring order that they should not go anywhere, she already decides emphatically, for the first time in her life: "*No, my dear mother. Not this time*! The word *no* had not yet been uttered but it already existed. It had already broken through like a puny shoot. She decided simply to face her mother with the fact of her family's disobedience without any preliminary discussion." (106, 107)

Arguably, the inner decision to say no is by no means an easy matter. For a woman long accustomed to the terrors and fears from both the outside totalitarian regime and the inside monarch, the lasting traumas and torments are beyond human imagination. It indeed takes great courage to persuade oneself to think, feel, behave, and act otherwise.

With the approach of the final hour, Anna cannot help imagining

the inevitable havoc her mother will wreck after their departure. However, she does not care about it that much any longer. Tracing back her history in this perverted mother-daughter relationship, the present change is indeed radical: forty years ago, Anna used to have the impulse to hit this beastly woman over the head with the furniture; thirty years ago, she would have liked to pull her hair. However, for a long time until now, all those hidden violent desires are largely repressed, and she begins to learn to take every harsh word lightly. Now, before she leaves, she finally regains the urge to show some disobedience and protest for every suffering she bears in the old woman's presence— "Suddenly she saw, as if it had already happened, herself—Anna—taking a long easy swing and giving that old rouged cheek a good hard long-overdue slap" (108, 109). She feels "a marvelously triumphant sense of freedom and victory." (109)

However, one wrong thing done by Anna turns the final great escape into a tragic disaster. The old woman seems to have sensed something, or simply makes the usual tiring demand for a bottle of milk. Had Anna refused to rush outside to buy the milk for her, nothing would have happened. But Anna does make a good calculation of time left for her to do all the chores and leave without being noticed. When she is back from the shop, in her great elation over her coming victory, she is hit by a car even without time to notice, and falls on the pavement, dead.

The death of Anna makes every hopeful plan become a thing of the past. This time should have been a time for mourning. But Mour seems to be unmoved. She continues to ask for everything, finally inviting a slap from Katya that should have been given by Anna. The description of this scene is as specific and vivid as possible: "Katya went over to Mour, took a long easy swing, and gave her old and yet unpainted cheek a good hard long-overdue slap." (110)

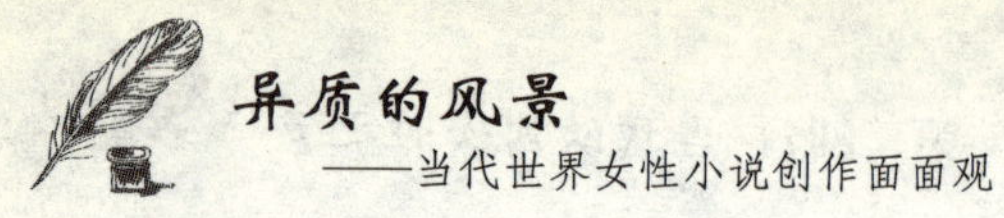

In a sense, this slap comes in a very timely way, and serves as a kind of revenge for Anna, who can no longer make this gesture. A granddaughter's revenge on her grandmother for her mother may sound alarming, but this is exactly what happens and necessarily happens in a dysfunctional society that is pervaded by power and desire, not love or humanity.

The response from Mour after receiving this slap offers nothing short of a shock, for she seems to gain a morbid sense of satisfaction and victory due to this tragedy—she "said, quietly and distinctly, 'What? What? All the same, everything shall be as I wish."(110)

Katya's response to Mour's remark is even more disheartening. The same rebellious girl who slaps the old dowager for her mother fails to run away with her children on the trip to Greece. Instead, she "walked past her to the kitchen, slit open the carton, and slopped the milk into the cold coffee"(110). Such an act amounts to the sheer futility of all previous attempts to escape the cage and prison. In the ultimate sense, they cannot break away the restrictions and controls of the power structures. The consciousness of freedom is there, but it is still in its infancy. It necessarily takes a much longer time for people who are already used to the terror of the authoritarian ideology to know, to act, and to be decisive.

Helena Goscilo argues, "Although at first glance Ulitskaya's stories resemble Petrushevskaya's in their gynocentrism and taboo-breaking, on a closer inspection, their unshakable faith in the significance and effectiveness of ethical behavior contrasts with Petrushevskaya's bleak conviction that people are fundamentally maimed and isolated in an alienated world." However, in "The Queen of Spades" and many other stories by Ulitskaya, strains of bleakness and hopelessness still run deep. This is not to simply refute Goscilo's argument, but to highlight the common and long-

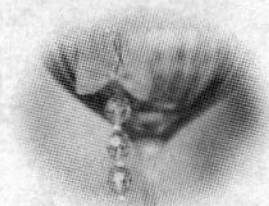

lasting traumas and sadness in their narrative focus that cannot be easily or neatly erased for post-Soviet-era citizens, especially women. Ulitskaya and Petrushevskaya may write in markedly different styles, yet basically they write the same script.

第八章　对完全结合的追寻

——读克罗地亚女作家斯拉芬卡·德拉库利奇的长篇小说《男人之味》

在创作与新闻报道方面都很成功的克罗地亚作家拉芬卡·德拉库利奇（1949—　）确实“不会让人失望”(《新政客》)。她最喜欢探讨的话题包括意识形态控制，意识形态控制对人类心智和思维方式的微妙影响，以及大胆的、打破禁忌的性。

在《男人之味》中，德拉库利奇充分显示了自己在纯粹性叙事方面的大师级功力。从表面上来看，这只是个杀人、分尸、抛尸的恐怖故事。然而，这本小说却不仅仅是简单的犯罪小说。它所隐藏的另外几个维度使我们这一最初的印象得以复杂化。

小说试图挖掘的第一个，也是最明显的维度便是对食人主义的理解。从一开始，男主人公——来自巴西的人类学家何塞就对这项研究表现出了强烈的兴趣。在他与自己的女朋友、女主人公——诗人特蕾莎的关系当中，一个重复出现的话题便是有关新、老食人主义的各种故事（本土印第安人、日本人佐川、在汤姆金斯的无家可归者)。在他们各种各样的讨论中，食人主义被以一种特别的方式得以理解：一种可以被道德和宗教证明合理性的神圣饥饿，一种仪式性的愉悦，一种将爱情永恒化的极端、决绝的姿态。

小说试图探索的另一个维度是偏执型的、吞没一切的身体交合。对于特蕾莎和何塞来说，这种纯粹的身体性也被以一种特别的方式得以理解：一种完全的结合，一种彻底的交流方式，向无用的语言发起挑战。触摸似乎就意味着一切。

隐藏在文本之中的还有一个维度，那就是死亡。在何塞和特蕾莎看来，死亡被诡异地认为是一种为了达到彻底交合、交流而必需的阶段。这是一种结束人生种种不确定性、种种两难困境的

手段。这也是他们的共识，一个通过细小的信号与动作达成的默认，其效力胜过任何书面性的协议。

正是这三种维度共同导致了特蕾莎对何塞的谋杀。事实上，这三种维度最终都指向了一个终极的存在性理由：对虚幻的“此时此地”的信念，认为它是可以对抗过去或将来、别处（不管是华沙还是圣保罗）的唯一现实。因此，小说的人物其实都活在一个没有希望的世界里，没有安全感，高度脆弱，一直都被充满创伤的过去所困扰。这就是为什么特蕾莎那么容易在很多情况下都变得神经兮兮的：那些她不熟悉的东西，譬如何塞的语言，习惯，还有他的孩子，都让她感到不安；那些把她排除在外的东西，譬如说何塞和他妻子、他人共有的过去，都让她难以忍受；何塞只离开了自己三天，特蕾莎便有些魂不守舍；特蕾莎为了找到何塞而实践的旧金山之行加深了她的恐惧；当何塞终于回到自己身边时，她又胡思乱想，总觉得他身上发生了微妙的变化。

对于一个杀人者来说，为自己的行为找到合理的借口是必经之旅。特蕾莎也不例外。之前谈到的三个维度，还有那个看似高深的终极原因，至少让她自己确信了这一行为的合理性。然而，在行动之时，她所有这些看似合理的理由都被解构了，而解构这一切的那个人就是特蕾莎自己。她精心构建的精神世界彻底被粉粹了。

首当其冲的便是那个食人主义。当特雷莎真的吃起自己爱人的肉时，她原先期待的那种仪式般的愉悦感立刻就烟消云散了。相反，她感到“好像自己的身体被什么机械的力量控制了一样，那力量比自己的意志强很多很多”(186)①。她对他身体的饥饿“和什么身体、心灵结合的仪式毫无关联，只是狂野的嚼肉欲望”(186)。从以上的叙事可以看出，在食人的过程中，绝对没有任何神圣可言。留下的只是像动物一般的丑恶与残忍。

---

① 本章所引依据 Slavenka Drakulić，*The Taste of a Man*，translated by Christina Pribichevich Zoric（London：Abacus，1997）. 引文后括号内的数字为引文在原著中的页码。

第二个被激烈解构的观念就是身体性的性行为。随着二人对彼此身体的贪欲加深，那种通过纯粹感官实现高级爱情理想的高谈阔论渐渐显现出仅仅是无根无据的胡说。从本质上来讲，这种身份行为、这种完全占有的关系，其实是在不智地复制着曾经肆虐波兰（特蕾莎的故乡）的专制现实。在占据权力之后，曾经遭受恐惧和其他创伤式体验的无权一方反而经常会变得更加残暴，更加非人性。在小说中，特蕾莎在成功掌控何塞之后对他的物化就可以充分证明这一点：何塞愈发变成了“东西、事物、物体”(165)。特蕾莎变成了拿着手术刀杀人的“医生”(164)，“监狱狱卒”(164)，“刽子手或职业杀手”(164)。不仅如此，这种肉体关系并没有进一步加深彼此的理解，只是让他们在最原始的层面上感受彼此的存在，更别提什么深层面上心与心的交流了。

把死亡作为达到最终结合之手段的信念，也不断受到严峻的考验。在她的杀人行为中，曾经认为自己这么做完全正确的特蕾莎开始发现自己也动摇了。她开始怀疑自己这么做到底对不对。在她的感觉里，有两股强大的力量——一是她冷静、理性的一面，一是她隐藏起来的疯狂一面——在把她向两个完全相反的方向拉。她不断地挣扎于歇斯底里的边缘。结果，她再也无法以任何冠冕堂皇的理由来证明何塞死亡的意义了。它越来越像是个烦人、累人的“任务”，根本就不能和那些高贵的追求相提并论。

最后被解构的、也是最重要的一个方面就是特蕾莎根本的人生观，即指导她人生、让她作出可怕行为的虚无主义。对于每个人来说，人生确实是悲剧性的。当下可能确实是我们能够把握的唯一存在。但是，这种悲观主义并不应该成为我们为自身利益伤害别人的理由。在一个陌生的土地上被双重隔离，特蕾莎确实有理由为这个世界、为自己伤感。然而，她本应该有足够的理智去明白，其他人的生活同样是悲剧性的，同样是伤感的。她要么故意无视这一事实，要么就是仅仅能意识到自己一个人的感受。从根本上来说，她是个非常自私和愚蠢的存在。也正是因为她的自私和愚蠢，才让她变得如此冷酷、无情。

Chapter 8 In Search of Absolute Union in Slavenka Drakulić 's *The Taste of a Man* (Croatia)

Equally successful as a writer and journalist, Croatian writer Slavenka Drakulić (1949—) is certainly someone who "does not disappoint" (*New Statesman*). Among her favourite subjects are the ideological control and its subtle influences on human minds and ways of thinking, as well as audacious, taboo-breaking sexuality.

In *The Taste of a Man*, Drakulić 's masterly accomplishment in narrating sheer sexuality in the purist sense is fully shown. On the surface, this is a story of brutal murder, dismemberment, and disposal of the remains. However, it is not simple crime fiction. Instead, it has several further dimensions that complicate this initial impression.

The first and most noticeable dimension the novel attempts to delve into is cannibalism. From the very start, the male protagonist——Brazilian anthropologist called Jose, is eager to make a study of this subject. Various stories of old and modern cannibalism (the native Indians, Sagawa, a homeless man in Tomkins) recur in the relationship between Jose and her girlfriend, the female protagonist, Polish poetess Tereza. In their various discussions, cannibalism is understood in a very special sense: sacred hunger that can be justified as an ethical or religiously endorsed way of survival, a ceremonial pleasure, or an extreme and radical gesture to eternalize love.

Another dimension the novel tries to explore is the obsessive and all-consuming physical consummation. For Tereza and Jose, this sheer bodily physicality is understood also in a special sense: an absolute union, a thorough way of communication that defies and challenges language with its utter futility. To touch seems to be everything.

Still another dimension hidden in the text is death, which is strangely believed to be a necessary transitional stage for Jose and Tereza to achieve total communion and communication. It is a way to put an end to all life's uncertainties and dilemmas. It is something that gets mutual consent, a tacit agreement through small signals and movements more trustworthy than any written pact.

Arguably, this is exactly all these three dimensions that combine to cause Tereza's murder of Jose. In fact, these three dimensions point to an ultimate existential reason: the belief in the illusory "here and now" as the only reality to counter the overwhelming fears for the past and the future, the elsewhere, be it Warsaw or Sao Paulo. Therefore, the characters in the novel inhabit a hopeless world, having no sense of safety, highly fragile, always haunted by the traumatic past. That's why Tereza is easily neurotic in many cases: those unfamiliar things, such as Jose's language, habits and children make her uneasy; those that exclude her presence, such as Jose's shared past memories of his wife and others, are unbearable to her; Jose's mere three days of absence deeply unsettles Tereza; Tereza's visit to San Francisco for hunting down Jose heightens her fear; when Jose is finally back, she surmises that she has noticed subtle changes that are taking place in him.

For a murderer, finding good excuses is a necessary step. Tereza is no exception. The three dimensions, as well as the seemingly profound ultimate reason, at least convince herself in her act. However, in the very act itself, all of her good excuses are

deconstructed by no one but herself. Her carefully-shaped mental world is shattered during that process.

The first deconstructive focus is concentrated on cannibalism. When Tereza eats the meat of her lover, her original expectation of ritualistic pleasure is no longer there. Instead, she feels "as though (her) body was being controlled by some mechanical power stronger than my own will" (186)①. Her hunger for his body had "nothing to do any more with the ritual of union in body and spirit, but rather was a wild desire to gorge myself on his meat"(186). As can be seen in the narrative about the practice of cannibalism, nothing sacred or holy remains during the process. What is left is sheer animalism.

The second thing that is subjected to fierce deconstruction is the bodily, physical sex. With the development of the two lovers' appetite for each other, the high-sounding talk of achieving the high ideal of love through pure senses is revealed to be nothing but groundless nonsense. In essence, this physical act, this totally possessive relationship, unwittingly reproduces the dictatorial and authoritarian reality that once plagued Poland, Tereza's homeland. After assuming power, the powerless party who used to suffer fear and other traumatic experiences, often becomes even about more cruel and inhuman. This is testified by Tereza's objectification of Jose after being secure in her control of him: Jose was increasingly turning into "an article, a thing, an object"(165). She turns into a life-killing "doctor"(164) with a sharp scalpel, a "prison guard" (164), an "executioner or hatchet man"(164). Furthermore, instead of furthering their understanding of each other, this physical

---

① Slavenka Drakulić, *The Taste of a Man*, translated by Christina Pribichevich Zoric (London: Abacus, 1997). Subsequent citations to this work are given as parenthetical page references in the text.

relationship only makes them feel each other's presence on the most primitive level, not to mention heart-to-heart appreciation of the inner things about each other.

As to the belief in death as a means of achieving the utmost union, it is also vigorously tested for its strength. In her killing act, Tereza, who used to think this is right in every sense, suddenly finds herself to be struggling with it as well. She begins to doubt about her belief and even about herself. She feels two magnetic forces—her calmer and rational side, and her hidden and insane side—pulling her in opposite directions. She is constantly on the verge of hysteria. As it turns out, Jose' s death cannot be justified on sublime grounds, for it becomes increasingly like a tiring "task", hardly as exciting as lofty things.

The last and most important thing to be dissected is Tereza's fundamental philosophy of life, namely nihilism that guides her life and contributes to her terrible actions. Life may indeed be tragic for everyone. The present may indeed be the only thing that we seem capable of grasping. But this pessimism should not become the reason for hurting others for our own interests. Doubly alienated in a strange land, Tereza does have reasons to feel sorry for this world and herself. But she should have had enough senses to know that others' lives are equally tragic and deeply sad. She either deliberately ignores this fact, or is simply unaware of others' feelings other than her own. Fundamentally, she is a very selfish and foolish being. It is nothing but her selfishness and foolishness that make her so cold and cruel.

第三部分
当代美洲女性之声

Part Three
Contemporary Female Voices from America

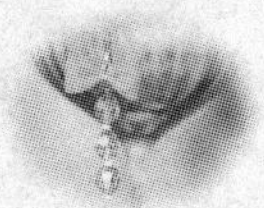

第九章　对男性单向思维快照式的揭示

——读美国女作家苏珊·米诺的短篇小说《打击》

在当今美国的女性作家中，颇受批评家青睐的作家苏珊·米诺（1956—　）占据了一个非常独特的位置，因为她能够观察到人类欲望和失落中最细微、最隐秘的细节，并且以看似简单的文笔加以讲述。

在《打击》中，米诺成功地向我们展示了一个失去爱情的男人在一个女性朋友（非女友）家里自发性的反应和行为举止，以微妙的方式揭示了他思维方式上的严重问题，还有他的欲望被挫败的真正原因。

从一开始，比尔就给读者一种粗鲁、自私的印象。他给他的女性朋友、叙事者“我”打电话的时间经常是“中午”(43)[①]，一个并不太适合打电话的时间。他似乎根本不考虑别人可能会有休息的需要。而当他知道朋友在家时，便忙不迭地飞奔到那里。当他的朋友终于打开门时，他的反应非常奇怪，甚至“往回跳了一下……是惊跳，有点像是要用提包保护自己似的”。(43) 所有这些姿态都让她有些无语。

接下来的情景甚至更加滑稽。比尔在走进朋友的公寓时，竟然“伸长了脖子，看看是不是有人藏在门铰链旁边”。(43) 这种鬼鬼祟祟、神神秘秘的行为有点偷窥的意味，一点都不符合作为客人应该遵守的礼貌。很明显，朋友对他的这种古怪行为已经司空

---

① 本章所引依据 Susan Minot，*Lust and Other Stories*（New York：Vintage Books，2000）. 引文后括号内的数字为引文在原著中的页码。

见惯，见怪不怪了。

当他们终于交谈时，比尔便直截了当地告诉了朋友自己今天的来意：自己与女朋友海伦分手了。他感觉自己被这个巨大的打击折磨得不行，连觉都睡不着，因此，他需要找个“什么地儿”(43)。这个“什么地儿”当然就是叙事者的公寓了。当他提出这个请求时，他简直就“像是个通缉犯”。(43)

尽管这只是个请求，比尔却并没把它当成是请求。他看起来已经想当然地认为，自己来就是为了征服一切的。在他的朋友还没说话之前，他就递给她一个塑料购物袋，里面装了几个礼物，目的当然是希望他能留下来住。在这些东西里面有一本是法文书，因为他“想当然地认为”(44)他的朋友是读法文的。事实上，她根本不是。这无异于表明，尽管比尔看起来很有心，其实根本不真正关心别人的兴趣，更别说正确地记下它们了。

在展示完自己的礼物之后，比尔便开始提出一个又一个的要求。首先，他要吃那些冰箱里没有的食物，接着又要给别人打电话。在一次电话中，叙事者“我”能清楚地看到“比尔看着我的脸，但却没看见我”(45)。在这次电话之后，比尔要求“我”保证他的隐私权，绝不能把他的行踪告诉给任何人。他甚至让叙事者告诉海伦（如果她真的问的话）她这里有个情人，不方便见客。

在比尔住下来的这段时间，这位女性朋友意味深长地笑了好几次。所有这些笑的表情——不管它们是“微笑”(45)，“露齿而笑”(45)，还是“面露喜色地笑”(46)，都是对比尔举止行为的一个无声、但却明白有力的评论。面对比尔的愚顽可笑，朋友只能包容再包容。当然，不能超过她的底限。现在，比尔的女朋友为何弃他而去，已经变得再清楚不过了。

有趣的是，在二人交谈的时候，比尔竟然对某天晚上陪叙事者“我”一起的朋友大肆点评。在他看来，“我”的这个电影摄影技师朋友“粗鲁”(45)，“古怪”(46)——“他们这些人就喜欢管着别人……这些男人的事情只有男人才懂。”(46)其实，把这个评

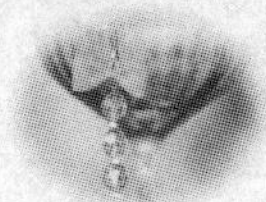

论安在他自己身上是最合适的，因为他才是那个粗鲁、古怪的家伙。米诺在这里运用的微妙反讽确实达到了预期效果。

当二人一起去博物馆时，让人忍无可忍的事情终于发生了。比尔偏爱伊斯兰艺术，而他的朋友对此却一无所知。然而，比尔似乎兴趣丝毫未减，仍然迫不及待地给她讲这讲那，尤其是关于狂欢宴会。他的讲授被形容为“强烈，但是毫无趣味”(47)，非常考验人的耐心。尽管他这些狂乱而又脆弱的情感，他讲东西时那种乏味的方式早已经“让我有点烦了”(47)，他还是不依不饶，没完没了，又开始说起了电影摄影技师的坏话。她情不自禁地回想起了他们俩过去差一点就在一起的日子。他曾经是那么稳重、那么“随和”(47)。然而，让她有些伤感的是，他现在完全变了一个人。

这篇短篇小说只是抓取了两个朋友生活中几个看似普通的事件，很多都是通过对话完成。然而，通过这位女性朋友敏锐地观察和适宜的脸部表情，一个自私、滑稽、经常有些粗鲁的男性漫画像就清楚地展现在了读者面前。从某种意义上来讲，这确实是对当代男性心态的一个很好反映，也说明单向度的男性沙文主义对于当今社会仍然残存的影响。

Chapter 9 A Snapshot Revelation of the Male One-dimensional Way of Thinking in Susan Minot's "Blow"(USA)

Among the contemporary women writers working in the United States, critically-acclaimed writer Susan Minot (1956—) takes up a quite unique position, for she has a unusual flair for observing the most minute and hidden details about human desire and loss, and telling them in deceptively simple prose.

In "Blow", Minot manages to show a deserted man's spontaneous responses and behaviours in a female friend's home, revealing in subtle ways his serious problems in ways of thinking, as well as the real reason why his desire is inevitably foiled.

From the very start, Bill leaves readers with an impression of rudeness and selfishness. He calls his female friend, the narrator "I" "in the middle of the day"(43)[①], hardly an appropriate time to make phone calls. He does not seem to care the least about other people's needs for a rest. When he knows his friend is at home, he arrives only two minutes later. When his female friend finally opens the door, he even "jumped back … startled, sort of shielding himself with his briefcase."(43) All these gestures make her quite speechless.

The following scene is even funnier. Before he comes into his female friend's apartment, Bill "craned his neck inside to check if anyone were hiding by the door hinges."(43) This secretive

---

① Susan Minot, *Lust and Other Stories* (New York: Vintage Books, 2000). Subsequent citations to this work are given as parenthetical page references in the text.

behaviour is a bit voyeuristic, hardly meeting the standard of politeness for a guest. The female friend is certainly long used to his weird behaviour like this.

When they finally talk to each other, Bill directly tells her about the purpose of his visit: the breakup between him and Helen, his girlfriend. He feels so tormented by this blow that he cannot sleep. He has to find "someplace"(43). This "someplace" is certainly the narrator's apartment. When he comes up with this demand, he is simply "like a hunted man"(43).

This request, despite its unmistakable nature as a "request", is not taken as a "request" by Bill. He seems to take it for granted that he comes, he conquers. Before his female friend can say anything, he hands her a plastic shopping bag in which there are a few things intended to be gifts to her for allowing him to stay. Among the things is a French book, for he "thought"(44) the friend reads French. In fact, she does not. This amounts to saying that despite his seeming thoughtfulness, Bill does not really care bout others' real interests, not to mention remembering them correctly.

After showing his gifts, Bill's ensuring demands come one by one. First, he demands food that is not kept in the fridge, followed by a demand for making calls. During a phone call, the friend "I" can clearly see "Bill looked at my face but through me"(45). After this call, Bill demands his privacy, asking her not to tell anyone about his stay. He even asks her to tell Helen (supposing she does ask) she has a lover here.

Throughout Bill's stay, the female friend smiles a few times. All these smiles—no matter it is "smile"(45), "grinning"(45), or "beaming"(46) —offer a silent and yet unmistakable and eloquent comment on Bill's behaviours. Faced with such idiocy and ridiculousness, the female friend can do nothing but tolerate, of course within a certain limit. The reason why Bill's girl friend has to abandon him also becomes crystal clear.

Interestingly, during their exchanges, Bill makes a comment on "my" friend who was with "me" the other night. In Bill's view, this cinematographer friend is "rude" (45) and "weird" (46) — "They like to control people… Men can tell these things about other men." (46) In fact, this comment is a very proper one for himself, for he is the truly rude and weird one. Minot's subtle irony does achieve its due effect.

The outrageous thing finally comes when they go to a museum together. Bill's favourite part is Islamic art, a completely alien thing to the female friend. However, Bill seems to have an unflagging interest in it, and cannot wait to lecture her about this and that, especially the orgies. His delivery is described as "intense, humourless" (47), a real test and challenge for patience. Despite the fact that his turbulent, easily fragile emotions and boring ways of telling things already "wear on me" (47), he certainly does not let "me" go and continue to say bad things about that cinematographer. She cannot help reminiscing their shared past when they were almost together. He used to be highly stable and "easygoing" (47). However, now, to her sadness, he is completely changed.

This short story captures several seemingly ordinary incidents in two friends' life together, mostly in dialogues. However, through the female friend's sharp observations and appropriate facial comments, a selfish, ridiculous and often rude male caricature is successfully revealed. In a sense, this is indeed a telling reflection of the contemporary male mentality and the lingering effect of one-dimensional male chauvinism even in modern times.

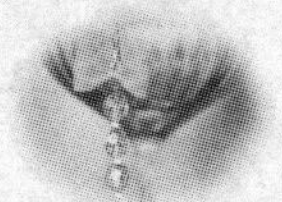

第十章 建立无法联系的联系

——读美国阿拉伯裔女作家阿丽亚·尤尼斯的短篇小说《黎巴嫩—底特律快车》

作为一个日渐崛起的声音，美国阿拉伯裔女作家阿丽亚·尤尼斯一直都以她“颇具想象力……感人至深、又非常有趣的”(《波士顿全球报》) 文学作品鼓舞、启发或者感动着我们。她的短篇小说《黎巴嫩—底特律快车》就是一个充分展现她独特叙事艺术的好例子。

首先让读者颇为震惊的便是它的“短”。在不到四页的篇幅内，这个故事却包含了大量的信息，有关美国、黎巴嫩，还有那些过着并不牢靠，但却也让他们受益良多的“双重生活”的阿拉伯裔美国人。很多人、很多风格、很多故事都在以迅疾但却并不容易让人忘记的方式发生着。

有趣的是，发生的桩桩件件并不显得随意或松散。在小说中，我们可以清楚地发现，一个无声，但却充当焦点的视角——那个叫易卜拉欣的老阿拉伯裔美国人——使这一切变为一个整体。确实，在整个小说的叙事过程之中，这位老者基本上都是处于无声的地位。然而，他却从来没有停止“看”或者说观察的行为。这就是他试图“掌控”自己生活的方式，这就是他试图理解周围世界的方式。以微妙但仍然可以被感知的方式，“看”(有时甚至接近于偷窥) 确实赋予了他某种权威，让读者注意到他不可质疑的存在。为了更清楚地展现他的存在，作者甚至把场景基本上局限在易卜拉欣乘坐的公交车上。毕竟，在公交车上，观察、看、思考都变成了高度有意义的行为。

沉静的易卜拉欣所做的第一个观察与美国有关。在他看来，这个“全新”的世界充满了太多的复杂性和矛盾性。一方面，这个国家似乎被各种各样的规则、命令、规定规约着，一切都强调着“准确性”、“不变性”。在整个叙事过程中，像“总是”(375)[①]、“必定”(375) 这样的词俯拾即是，随处可见。甚至那些生活在这里的人身上也有了“准确”的标记，不论是公交车司机、他自己，还是他女儿。然而，另一方面，这个国家同样也充斥着各种不守规矩、拒绝准确的生活方式。譬如，易卜拉欣在公交车上遇到的性感女郎就大胆地露出刺有纹身的肚脐。对于易卜拉欣来说，这种全新的、实验性的、打破成规的行为，这种“身体书写”确实令人很不安。除此之外，成长在这片土地上的儿子也和很多叛逆青年一样，养成了吸毒的坏习惯。美国的两面性让他陷入了极度的混乱之中。

易卜拉欣的第二个观察与第一个紧密相关，那就是，他开始感觉或者幻想：黎巴嫩——他的“故国”或许可以成为矫正美国混乱一面的对抗性力量。他情不自禁地开始怀念自己在“彼处”的过去。毕竟，那里代表着与“此处”迥然不同的一切。在“彼处”，他还是个被妈妈疼爱的孩子；“彼处”有山，有无花果，有果酱，还有自己的母亲；他的根，他的族裔身份，他的家庭身份，他的归属感，他“曾经”的一切，都被静静地、永恒地埋在了那里。这就是为什么他会叹息地说“今天已经离他的童年很远很远了。”(375)

他做的第三个，也是最重要的观察颇为复杂，那就是，他发现自己急切地要去“连接”那基本上“不可能连接”的过去和现在、旧与新，希望把它们连成一个可理解的整体。这已经在小说的标题“黎巴嫩—底特律快车”中有所暗示。是否真的有这么一辆快车，当然不是问题所在。真正重要的是能指背后的“所指”：那种希望把两个基本上无法调和的东西“直接”联系起来的欲望，不管这欲望有多么不现实。

---

① 本章引用依据 *Dinarzad's Children：An Anthology of Contemporary Arab American Fiction*，edited by Pauline Kaldas and Khaled Mattawa（Fayetteville：The University of Arkansas Press，2009）. 引文后括号内的数字为引文在原著中的页码。

在 33 号公交车上，易卜拉欣开始了狂“看”之旅，看的对象包括各行各业的人。经过第六大道与华盛顿街道时，他总是能窥视到那个老在家里看黄片的美国肥男。肥男的这一行为唤起了他压抑已久的、对他黎巴嫩岁月时一个“村里的女孩”的性幻想；住在另外一个房子里的、用过氧化氢漂白过头发的金发女郎，则让他想起了他生命中两个重要的、但是已经失去了（很大程度上是因为他自己的问题）的存在。这个女郎的年龄让他想到了自己已经被关到戒毒所的儿子，而她的模样则让他想到了自己的前妻；在他头上飞的飞机让他想起了自己的女儿和其他孩子，她们很可能就在飞机上；甚至过马路的小女孩也让他联想到了自己的外孙女。一句话，他偶遇的任何一个陌生人都变成了重要的存在。

狂“看”指向的东西很简单，但也很让人不安：他极度的孤独。身边毫无亲人，健康与青春也在逝去，留下来的也就只有幻想和想象。他需要看，需要思考，需要想象，只有这样才能够让自己的孤寂生活坚持下去。

唯一一个不是想象出来的人就是他的第二任妻子阿玛娜。当车流在沃伦和谢弗处慢下来的时候，他确实亲眼看到了她。然而，让我们惊讶的是，连这个仅存的浪漫情节也被打破了。确实，二人现在其实在各过各的日子，在有任何需要的时候只有自己可以依靠。这里的“拐棍”具有高度的象征意义。原来，到了生命的结束，每个人可以凭依的，也只有自己的拐棍。

在小说的最后，我们终于知道了公交车之旅的终点：机场。从阿姆斯特丹飞来的 KLM 247 航班会降落在这里。易卜拉欣现在已经不能、也不愿意再去海外旅行了。他来机场的目的其实是“看”他那些从黎巴嫩、约旦一路来到这里的阿拉伯同胞营造的感人场景。这些场景，不管是哭泣还是拥抱，都能让他把过去与现在、“彼地”与“此地”“连接”在一起。在这一时刻，他“真的”可以看到、闻到、感受到自己不争的存在和过去的自我。

无情的结尾再一次把这个自我意淫的梦彻底打破。当易卜拉欣想拉车绳下站时，他的听力暂时性地出了问题。他对黎巴嫩四季的理解也大有问题。易卜拉欣在下车前，与司机寒暄了几句，但是他发现，司机的多元文化（融合）论根本就毫无用处；而易卜拉欣不知道、我们却清楚知道的是，他本人的多元文化（融合）论也同样不可行。在无法调和的两方找到联系固然勇敢、感人，但是更多时候却会最终失败。易卜拉欣最后说的话甚至颇有些存在主义的味道："他想，要么我们死了，要么我们就得在哪个地方变老。"(378) 这里说的"哪个地方"事实上"哪里也不是"。正如他描述自己女儿境况时所说的那样，他自己其实也是"毫无进展"(376)。他是个希望通过连接过去和现在、连接过去生活与现在生活的人，希望"什么都是"，但最后他只是沦为了"什么都不是"的人。这就是一个背井离乡的阿拉伯美国人的命运。这也是有关流放与无根本身的一个宿命论式的隐喻。

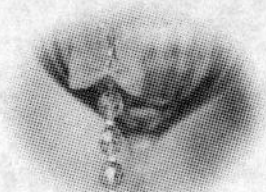

Chapter 10 Making Unconnectable Connections in Alia Yunis's "The Lebanon-Detroit Express"(USA)

As an emerging voice that steadily and swiftly builds her reputation for her "wonderfully imaginative ... poignant, hilarious" (*The Boston Globe*) literary output, Arab American fictional writer Alia Yunis never fails to inspire, enlighten or move us. Her short story "The Lebanon-Detroit Express" offers a telling example of her unique narrative art.

The first thing that strikes any reader is its short length. Within no more than four pages, the story still manages to include a huge load of information about America, about Lebanon, and the Arab Americans that lead a precarious and yet enriching "double life". Many people, many lifestyles, many stories do happen in fleeting and yet memorable ways.

Interestingly, these various happenings are not provided randomly or loosely. There is clearly a silent and yet arguably focal point of view that makes them into one whole, namely that of the old Arab American man called Ibrahim. Ironically, throughout the short story, except a few words at the end, he is largely silent and voiceless. However, he never ceases the act of "seeing" or observing. This is his way of trying to "control" his own life, of understanding the world around him. In subtle and yet palpable ways, "seeing"(sometimes verging on voyeurism) does empower him, making us readers aware of his undoubted presence. To make his presence more clear or conspicuous, the author even limits the setting largely to a bus that Ibrahim takes. After all, on a bus, observing, seeing, thinking become highly useful acts.

The first observation Ibrahim silently makes concerns his adopted land that is America. In his eyes, this "new" world is full of complexities and contradictions. On the one hand, this country seems to be guided by various rules, orders, regulations that put much emphasis on "exactness", on "changelessness". Throughout the narrative, words and phrases like "always" (375)[①], "without fail" (375) are very constant and highly visible, hardly needing us to notice them with care. Even the people that live here have borne the marks of "exactness", including the bus driver, him, and his own daughter. On the other hand, this same country is also a place that is guided by anything that goes against the orderly, exact way of life. For instance, the sexy young woman Ibrahim meets on the bus wears a pierced belly button that reveals a tattoo. For Ibrahim, this new, experimental, and norm-breaking behaviour, this "bodily writing" is disturbing. What's more, his son who grows up in this land has also developed the terrible habit of taking drugs like many rebelling youths here. The two-sidedness of America throws Ibrahim into utter chaos, utter confusion.

The second observation Ibrahim makes is closely related to the first one, that is, he starts to feel or fantasize that Lebanon, his "old" home country, may offer a countering force to correct every confusion arising in the US. He cannot help reminiscing about his past "there". After all, it represents everything that is markedly different from "here". "There", he is still a young child adored by his mother;

① *Dinarzad's Children: An Anthology of Contemporary Arab American Fiction*, edited by Pauline Kaldas and Khaled Mattawa (Fayetteville: The University of Arkansas Press, 2009). Subsequent citations to this work are given as parenthetical page references in the text.

"there" is where the mountains, fresh figs, jam, and his mother lie. His root, his racial identity, his domestic identity, his belongingness, and his everything that "used to be" are buried silently and eternally. That's why he sighs by saying "Today was a long time and a world away from his boyhood." (375)

The third, and the most important observation he makes is a complex one, that is, he finds himself eager to make the desperate attempt to "connect" the largely "unconnectable" past and present, old and new into an accessible and understandable whole. This is already implied in the title of the story "The Lebanon-Detroit Express". Whether there is such an express train or not is certainly not the issue here. What is important is the "signified" behind this signifier: the desire, no matter how unrealistic it is, to do the "direct" connecting between the two largely irreconcilable things.

On the No. 33 bus, Ibrahim goes on a "seeing" spree that covers people from all walks of life. The seedy porn-watching behaviour of the American fat man on Sixth and Washington arouses his long repressed sexual fantasies of his Arab "girl in the village" back in his Lebanese days; the peroxide blonde living in another house reminds him of two important and yet lost (largely because of his own faults) presences in his life: her age reminds him of his now rehabbed son, and her looks reminds him of his ex-wife; the airplanes that fly above him calls on his memories of his daughter and other children, who may be aboard them; even a little girl crossing the road conjures in his mind the image of his granddaughter. In a word, every stranger he meets by chance becomes an important presence.

What the "seeing" spree points to is simple and yet disturbing: his extreme loneliness. With no one around him, with health and youth lost on him, what is still left is vision and imagination. He needs to see, to think, to imagine in order to sustain his lonely life.

The only thing that is not imaginary is Amana, his second wife, whom he does see in person when the traffic slows at Warren and Schaeffer. However, to our surprise, even this remaining romantic plot is already shattered. They lead their separate lives, having themselves alone to rely upon whenever in need. The "cane" here is highly symbolic. Until the end of their life, each one can only cling to his or her own cane.

In the last page, we finally know the destination of the bus tour: the airport where the KLM flight 247 from Amsterdam will arrive. He is unable and unwilling to make any overseas travel elsewhere. The purpose of his going there is still to "see" all those moving scenes created by his fellow Arabs, who come here all the way from Lebanon and Jordon. These moving scenes, including weeping and embracing, can help him "connect" the past and the present, "there" and "here". He can "really" see, smell, and feel his own undoubted presence and his old self at this time.

The relentless ending again shatters this self-indulged dream into pieces. When Ibrahim pulls the cord for the bus to stop, his hearing is temporarily impaired. His understanding of the seasons in Lebanon is also left in question. When he exchanges pleasantries with the bus driver before leaving the bus, Ibrahim finds his multi-culturalism to be so much in vain; what Ibrahim does not know, and what we as readers know is the equal futility of his multi-culturalism on his part. Making connections between irreconcilable things is a brave and moving act. However, it, more often than not, tends to fail eventually. Arguably, the last words uttered by Ibrahim even assume a hopelessly existential status: "Either we die, he thought, or we get to be old somewhere." (378) The "somewhere" here is nothing but "nowhere". As he describes his daughter's condition, he

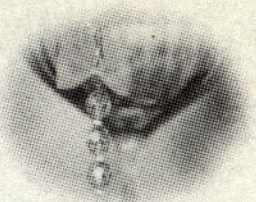

himself is also “not… going anywhere” (376). He is somebody who tries to be “both” by connecting his past and present, his old life and his new life, but he ends up being “neither…nor”. This is the fate of an exiled Arab American man. This is also the fatalistic metaphor of exile and rootlessness themselves.

第十一章　政治与性的倒置

——读美国华裔女作家李翊云的短篇小说《内布拉斯加公主》

在当今所有华裔美国作家当中，李翊云（1972—　）成功地占据了一个能见度颇高的位置。尽管她不论在语言还是文化方面都是半路出家，但却在这片土地上赢得了许多著名的奖项，还主持了许多重要的文学比赛。有趣、但也不无讽刺的是，她的文本却处处显得轻描淡写：她叙事的风格拒绝表面的戏剧化，她的文字在初读之后几乎不会对读者产生直接的影响。她笔下的男男女女似乎也不是高度个性化的、一看便能记住的存在。她也很少会给她作品的结尾抹上所谓“完美的一笔”。对于许多读者来说，她的结尾是模糊的、未完成的。

其实，李翊云的魅力本来就不在于她作品能产生的直接效果，而是超越、深潜于语言表征本身。她以非尝试的姿态所做的尝试其实是向我们展现一个深藏于内、未被言说、不可言说，但又明显在场、改变生命的东方哲学。这种哲学将当代政治关怀、性别关怀与普遍意义上的人性关怀交织成一个整体。《内布拉斯加公主》便是反映她独特叙事艺术的一个很好的样本。它通过对三个主人公生活的描述，探讨了他们共同的政治失语、性别错乱，还有对人生强烈的虚无感，以及他们代替直接话语宣示的各种行为。

在这篇小说里，并不算友好的意识形态——国家机器显得格外高调。不无讽刺意味的是，博深这个明显是最为可靠、最温顺的人却成了这种力量不断运作的场域。他先是被他工作的医院赶了出去，接着又在新的工作场所——首都的一个私人诊所被秘密警察监管、监视。最后，他不得不离开首都，却又在老家被软禁于家中。当他终于来到美国时，这种噩梦般的生活才告结束。

意识形态政治与性别管制经常是联系在一起的。在这篇小说里，对于博深来说，与政治失语紧密相连的是他对同性恋权利的疾呼（即使是以非公共性的方式）。当他所有表达他们作为同性恋（还有他自己）权利的尝试失败之后，他便转向了更加个人化的表达方式，交了个姓杨的男朋友。

当然，和博深相比，杨，也就是那个“内布拉斯加公主”，明显是个更加复杂的人物，很难用性别管制手段来加以控制、限制。从他很小的时候，他所学京剧里的男旦传统便已经让他分不清楚自己是男是女。他也经常会遭受他人将其看成是女性“他者”的、掠夺性的凝视。他似乎也习惯了这样的生活，甚至如法炮制，先勾引了博深作自己忠实（甚至有些盲目忠实）的爱人，然后又和自己都不怎么熟悉、更别提有什么爱情的女人萨莎有了孩子。除此之外，他自己还不洁身自好，一次次地出卖自己的身体。不无讽刺的是，他这种不负责任的方式并不是只有消极意义，因为它至少把萨莎与博深这两个可怜人的命运连在了一起。二人打算一起把孩子带大，“在外人看来，他们就像是最平常不过的父母一样”(90)①。从某种意义上说，确保这个孩子在新大陆的幸福也是一种颇具颠覆性的行为。

在整个故事里，意识形态控制与性别监管无所不在，然而都被以微妙或者直接的方式颠覆掉了。在解剖这些敏感议题时，李翊云确实证明了自己是个有极大潜力的个中好手。迄今为止，还没有一个亚裔美国作家像她这样写作。这本身就使得她显得与众不同，也证明了她持久的叙事能力。

① 本章所引依据 Yiyun Li, *A Thousand Years of Good Prayers* (New York: Random House, 2005). 引文后括号内的数字为引文在原著中的页码。

Chapter 11 Political and Sexual Inversions as Subversive Acts in Yiyun Li's "The Princess of Nebraska" (USA)

Among all contemporary Chinese American fiction writers active today, Yiyun Li (1972—) manages to secure a conspicuous and highly visible place. Despite her adopted status in both language and culture, she has won many prestigious prizes and chaired many key literary contests. Interestingly and even ironically, her writing nevertheless seems so understated in every sense: her narrative style is by no means dramatic, hardly making an immediate impact after reading at one sitting. Neither are her characters, male or female, highly recognizable as unique beings. Seldom does she offer a neat or so-called "perfect touch" to her endings, which seem to be vague and unresolved to many readers.

In fact, Yiyun Li's appeal does not lie in its immediate effect, but goes beneath and beyond the superficial marker of language. What she attempts, in a subtle gesture of non-attempting, to drive home is a hidden, unspoken, unspeakable, and yet obviously present life-transforming eastern philosophy of life that intertwines contemporary political concerns, gender concerns and universally human concerns into one whole. "The Princess of Nebraska" offers an eloquent example to her unique narrative art, discussing political aphasia, confusion in gender, and a strong sense of nothingness in life in all three main characters' life, as well as the various actions they make as alternative means of vocal utterance.

In this short story, less-than-friendly ideological apparatus does assume a highly visible presence. Boshen, obviously the most trustworthy and docile man in this story, ironically becomes a constant site for the working of this force. He is first politely driven away from the hospital where he works, only to be constantly supervised and spied on by secret police in his second working place—a small private clinic in the capital. Eventually, he is forced to leave the capital and put in house arrest in his home town. Only when he makes his safe escape to America, is the nightmarish life in China over.

Ideological politics and gender policing are, more often than not, interrelated. In the short story, what is closely connected to the political aphasia for Boshen is his advocacy (even if it is private and non-public) of gay rights, greatly displeasing the authorities in power. When all his attempts to voice their (as well as his own) rights fail, he turns to a more personal way of expressing this view on gender by having Yang as his boyfriend.

Of course, compared to Boshen, Yang, the "princess of Nebraska", is arguably a more complex figure, harder to be contained and confined by gender policing. The *Nan Dan* Peking Opera tradition that fosters him from his early age almost contributes to his confusion over his own gender. He is so constantly subject to predatory gaze as a female "Other" that he even makes a career of it, first ensnaring Boshen as his faithful lover even in blind ways; fathering the child of a woman called Sasha that he barely knows, not to mention loving; prostituting himself again and again. Ironically, this irresponsible way of doing things is by no means completely negative, for it does manage to connect Sasha and Boshen together, who intend to raise his child together just "like the most ordinary couple to strangers"(90)[①]. In a sense, to ensure the happiness of this child in this new land is a further subversive act.

Throughout this short story, ideology control and gender policing are pervasive, and yet they are both subtly or directly subverted. In dissecting these sensitive issues, Yiyun Li is indeed already a well seasoned master with great potentials. So far, no other Asian American writer writes about them in similar ways, which alone sets her well apart and proves her enduring narrative strength.

① Yiyun Li, *A Thousand Years of Good Prayers* (New York: Random House, 2005).

第十二章 作为控制手段的偷窥癖

——读加拿大女作家艾丽丝·门罗的短篇小说《我一直打算告诉你的一些事》

三获加拿大总督文学奖的作家艾丽丝·门罗（1931— ）现今已成为短篇小说领域的世界级大师。《休斯敦邮报》这样评价她：她“有力地捕捉到了人性多变冲动中的人性本质……很难想象谁有比她更迅捷的感知力。”她作品当中的那些姐妹、母女、阿姨、祖母、朋友都确实充满了情感和智识上的复杂性，在一个深刻的层面上展示了嫉妒、权力、控制欲望的运作。

在《我一直打算告诉你的一些事》中，门罗成功地塑造了一对姐妹花，她们从一开始便处于很紧张的关系当中。妹妹埃塔没完没了地夸赞姐姐莎尔的前男友布莱基·诺贝尔，说他如何如何魅力无敌，似乎要故意引起姐姐的隐痛或不安。她在说这些话的同时，还以“虐待狂”般的方式观察她紧张的反应，借以实现自我满足。

在接下来的倒叙中，埃塔与莎尔那古怪的、近乎让人无法理解的交流方式似乎变得愈加清晰。原因其实就在于埃塔对自己姐姐的美貌、能获取两个男人爱情的能力发自内心、根深蒂固的嫉妒。她必须要找到其他的方式来控制自己的姐姐，以此作为报复。最终，她决定，最好的方式便是做个一生的偷窥者。在偷窥之后，她便可以自由地把手中掌握的信息告诉或者不告诉给相关的人，以达到最为邪恶的结果。

三十五年来，这个偷窥者不知疲惫地隐藏在暗处，不断地观察着其他人（尤其是她姐姐）的行为与面部表情。当莎尔与布莱基做爱时，她竟然将光照到他们赤裸的身体之上，让他们惊惧、逃离。然而，事后，她竟然又告诉姐姐自己什么都没有看到。这种假装的清纯反而会让莎尔更加恐惧。当莎尔知道布莱基最终要娶的是别人、而不是自己时，她尝试着自杀。这也变成了埃塔的秘密，成为了她控制自己姐姐的微妙资本。当莎尔知道自己与布莱基未来无望时，终于嫁给了学校老师亚瑟·康博。然而，她的内心是不幸福的。这又成为了埃塔可以操纵的有用信息。她故意把莎尔打扮得非常花哨，这自然引来周围人对莎尔的批评，纷纷责备她不合身份的穿着。现在，在埃塔精心的计划下，莎尔婚姻的脆弱性终于为世人所知。

很多年后，当布莱基重返小镇之时，埃塔控制姐姐的机会再次到来，这也是最可怕的一次机会。莎尔与他旧情复燃，这让埃塔再次恼怒不已，因为嫉妒的她又看到了他们幸福的模样。她决定一劳永逸地毁掉它。这回，她讲了两次故事。第一次，她趁布莱基不在的几天，跑到莎尔那里，跟她撒了一个谎，说她珍视了这么久的情人又出去结婚去了，跟上次一样。这无异于是再次揭开了莎尔的旧伤疤。她做的第二件事便是把旧事跟亚瑟说了。这次，已经饱受严重创伤的莎尔终于突发心脏病死去。在某种程度上来讲，其实是埃塔的嫉妒、还有她对莎尔生活的秘密掌控最终导致了莎尔的死亡。这死亡看似突发，其实是个慢性中毒的过程。

现在，埃塔终于成功地报复了自己的姐姐。莎尔的死使她再也不能与布莱基有什么暧昧了，也使得她和亚瑟的婚姻解体了。在姐姐永远的缺席之下，埃塔的存在终于被注意到了。确实，她姐姐的葬礼不久，她和亚瑟便开始交往起来，直到最后住在了一起。埃塔做饭，二人一起吃饭，好像其乐融融的样子。正如叙事者嘲讽的评论那样，“如果他们结婚了，别人会说他们真的很幸福。”(23)①

---

① 本章所引依据 Alice Munro, *Something I've Been Meaning to Tell You* (New York: Vintage Books, 2004). 引文后括号内的数字为引文在原著中的页码。

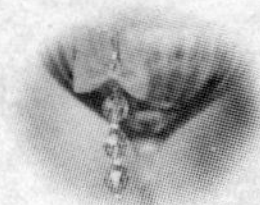

这一“幸福”的状态确实问题多多，因为它是多年操纵、控制甚至是故意伤害的结果。埃塔得到了她想要的东西，也除掉了她痛恨的东西。然而，当不再有她通过偷窥而加以控制的客体时，她却感到了迷茫和不适。在告诉、推迟告诉了多次之后，终于轮到她把自己做过、想过的种种行径告诉亚瑟。这就是为什么“有时候埃塔话到嘴边，想告诉亚瑟：‘我一直打算告诉你一些事。’”(23) 然而，埃塔永远也不可能勇敢地道出真相，因为那必然会让她失去现在的生活，也意味着之前的努力全部白费。因为，她几乎是永远地失去了倾诉、忏悔的可能。对于门罗来说，这个结尾算得上是以颇具讽刺性的方式帮助莎尔报了仇。她曾经在她妹妹的告诉与不告诉行为中深受其害，现在也轮到她妹妹来尝一尝其中的滋味了。

Chapter 12 Voyeurism as a Means of Control in Alice Munro's "Something I've Been Meaning to Tell You" (Canada)

Thrice Governor's Literary Award winner, Alice Munro (1931—) has already become a global phenomenon in the field of short stories. According to *Houston Post*, she has a "trenchant ability to capture the essence of personality in the vagaries of human impulses... It is hard to imagine a perception more acute." Arguably, the sisters, mothers and daughters, aunts, grandmothers, and friends in her works are indeed full of emotional complexity and intellectual unintelligibility that reveal on a profound level the workings of jealousy, power and the will to control.

In "Something I've Been Meaning to Tell You", Munro successfully creates two sisters whose relationship seems to be somewhat strained from the very start. The younger sister Et seems to be deliberately provoking her older sister Char's sadness or unease by mentioning her ex-lover called Blaikie Noble, praising his unbeatable charm in a lavish manner. When saying this, Et "sadistically" watches her nervous reaction for personal satisfaction.

In the following flashback, Et's weird and hardly intelligible (in a normal sense) way of communicating with her own sister seems to be clearer. The reason lies in Et's deep-seated jealousy of her sister's beauty and ability to win two men's love. She has to seek out other ways to control her sister as a sort of revenge. She finally decides that the best way for her is to be a lifetime voyeur. After

that, she can freely withhold or tell the information in her hands to those people concerned so as to achieve the most vicious end.

For thirty-five years, this voyeur untiringly lurks in the dark, constantly observing other people's actions and expressions on their faces, especially those of her sister's. When Char makes love to Blaikie, she turns on the light to reveal their naked bodies, making them fall into great panic and run away. However, later, she even tells her sister that she has not seen anything. This feigned innocence can only heighten Char's fear. When her sister knows that Blaikie is going to marry someone else, she attempts to kill herself. This knowledge also becomes Et's secret and subtle asset for controlling her sister. When Char knows the impossibility of any more future with Blaikie, she finally marries the school teacher Arthur Comber. However, inwardly, she is not really happy. This again becomes useful knowledge for Et to manoeuvre. She deliberately keeps her sister dressed in a too showy manner, thus inviting other people's criticism of Char for such an improper way of dressing. The vulnerability in Char's marriage is now made fully public, all thanks to Et's tireless plan.

The most terrifying chance for Et to control her sister arrives when Blaikie returns to town after many years. The old romance between Char and him inevitably revives. This infuriates Et again, who jealously watches their happiness. She intends to destroy it once and for all. This time, she does her storytelling twice. In Blaikie's absence for a few days, she first rushes to tell a lie to Char, saying that this lover she has cherished for such a long time has left to get married, just like before. This amounts to ripping off the old wounds again. The second thing she does is to tell the old story minus Char's suicide attempt to Arthur. At this time, the seriously traumatized Char suddenly dies from a fatal heart attack. In a way, it is Et's jealousy and secret control of her life that finally leads to her death. It looks sudden, but in fact a slowly poisoned one.

Now, Et finally succeeds in fulfilling her revengeful expectations. The death of Char makes her affair with Blaikie impossible any more, and also makes her marriage with Arthur void. In her sister's eternal absence, her presence starts to be noticed. Indeed, not long after her sister's funeral, she and Arthur begin their love affairs and eventually live together. Et does the cooking, and they eat together, as if very happily. Just as the narrator wryly comments, "If they had been married, people would have said they were very happy."(23)①

This "happy" state is indeed problematic, for it is the result of many years of manoeuvre, controlling, and even deliberate hurting. Et gets what she wants, and gets rid of what she hates. However, when there is no one as the object for her to control through her voyeurism, she feels both lost and dis-eased. After telling and delaying telling things, it is finally her turn to tell Arthur about herself, about her wicked deeds and thoughts. That's why "(s) ometimes Et had it on the tip of her tongue to say to Arthur, 'There's something I've been meaning to tell you.'"(23) However, Et can never be brave enough to do the telling, for that necessarily involves the loss of her present life and her failure in all previous manoeuvres. Therefore, she is almost eternally deprived of the right to tell. For Munro, this ending may serve as an ironic way to avenge Char who has suffered so much from her sister's telling and non-telling.

---

① Alice Munro, *Something I've Been Meaning to Tell You* (New York: Vintage Books, 2004). Subsequent citations to this work are given as parenthetical page references in the text.

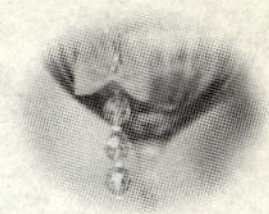

第十三章 颠覆传统女性气质与书写本身的“女性书写”

——读巴西女作家克拉丽斯·利斯佩克托的长篇小说《星光时刻》

对于著名的法国女权主义批评家埃莱娜·西苏来说，巴西作家克拉丽斯·利斯佩克托（1920—1977）绝对算是一个不折不扣的大发现。她的作品被认为是真正的“女性书写”。利斯佩克托的文风确实非常特别，很难被人轻易模仿。它微妙地混合了小说与哲学的元素，并让叙事者和人物进行创造性的互动。这些特点使得全世界的读者都为之一振。

在她完美的绝笔之作——《星光时刻》一书中，利斯佩克托塑造了两个非常独特的形象——罗德里戈和玛卡贝娅，他们身上都标有她独特的风格。前者有双重身份，既是叙事者，又是小说中的人物。从一开始，这个大都市人的形象便是在多个层面上自相矛盾、不可靠的。他不断地质疑自己（觉得自己不擅长描述事物），甚至问自己为什么要写玛卡贝娅，为什么要写她那个缺乏深度的故事。因此，他的叙述不可避免地陷入到停停续续、续续停停的状态。当他的叙事看起来终于比较稳定、看似有些逻辑的时候，他便跟读者宣称，自己会确保公正、客观，即使为此付出情感贫瘠的代价也在所不惜。然而，他却一次又一次地陷入自己的情绪之中。在讲述玛卡贝娅故事的整个过程之中，他从未停止评论，也从未停止展示他自己的创作过程。他甚至经常把玛卡贝娅的生活与自己的生活相比。他也跟读者宣称，自己要写一个简单的故事，有清楚的开头、中间部分和结尾。然而，他的开头却写得冗长无比，故事迟迟无法正式开始；中间部分也是被弄得支离破碎，不断打断正常的叙事；结尾也是迟迟不到，一次次被编辑、重写。当玛卡贝娅终于死了的时候，他甚至感觉自己也死了，宛如是对罗兰·巴特“作者已死”的回应。

小说的中心人物玛卡贝娅尽管看起来很简单，其实是个比罗德里戈更复杂的建构。在整个文学史上，这个人物是前所未见的。她来自巴西东北部的贫民窟，一生下来便是一身的不幸：贫穷、愚蠢、口齿不清、丑陋、双目无神，几乎不识字，没人知道她，也没人看得到她。不仅如此，没人想要她，没人需要她，没人爱她。终其一生，她在社会上得到的最好的职位先是个默默无闻的打字员，然后是个金属制造工。

让读者震惊的是，她在如此恶劣环境下神奇的回弹能力。她的内心是自由的。对于自由的真谛，她有一种少有的、直觉性的、无意识的理解力。她似乎在无意识地遵循着自己构建的“我在，故我在”(36)[①] 原则。在她眼里，能够活着本身便已经够棒了。她真的是非常开心，开心得就像是个白痴，从来都没有意识到自己的不幸状况。她甚至想做一个像玛丽莲·梦露一样的电影明星。尽管她什么都没有，却有着强烈的信念。这种信念从严格意义上来说并不是宗教性的，但是却一样强烈，一样坚定。她总是问些看起来很琐碎、和她毫无关系的问题。她从来不过分担心自己的将来。和她的情人奥利皮科、工友格洛里亚不同，她的阶级意识非常模糊，她从来没想过要去加入什么所谓的特权阶层，从来没有意识到自己只是资本主义机器齿轮上的一个“齿牙”(29)。

即使在被奥利皮科抛弃、背叛、伤害之后，她仍然没有感到绝望。事实上，她继续自己的生活，就像什么都没有发生过一样。突然，她脑中迸出一个想法——既然没人爱她，她应该请自己吃饭！她甚至开始给自己涂上大量的口红。从某种程度上来说，这

① 本章所引依据 Clarice Lispector，*The Hour of the Star*，translated by Giovanni Pontiero（New York：New Directions，1992）. 引文后括号内的数字为引文在原著中的页码。

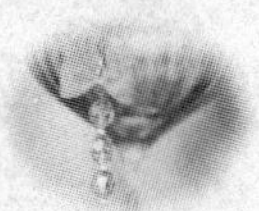

是她女性意识的开始。

不无讽刺的是，对于玛卡贝娅来说，让她的人生发生彻底转变的真正转折点与一直拒绝她的语言文字有关。她“一生存在的高潮”便是与卡洛塔夫人（一个传奇性的人物，先做妓女，后来做了妓院老板，最后做了占卜师）具有决定性意义的邂逅。她对自由真意的理解，上升到了一个有意识的层面。当卡洛塔夫人为她占卜命运时，先让她用左手把牌分成几份，一切就绪之后，她便开始占卜。她一边占卜，一边惊叫：“你怎么会活得这么悲惨!”(75) 她接着说：“至于说你眼前的将来，那同样悲惨。你会失去你的工作，就像你已经失去你的男友一样。”(75，76)

然而，过了一会儿，卡洛塔夫人又突然告诉玛卡贝娅，她的命运出现了转机。她将变成一个全新的人；她的男朋友会后悔自己之前的抛弃行为，回到她身边；她的老板会改变主意，希望她继续留下来工作；一个叫汉斯的外国绅士也会突然将自己的财产赠予她。这个预言让她产生了前所未有的、对未来强烈的渴望和希冀。她感到自己面对无限的可能性。她的时刻终于来临了。不无讽刺的是，在她激动地发现了现在与未来的联系时，她也终于意识到，自己一直以来的生活确实是不幸的。

这个从来不缺乏戏剧性元素的叙事以一个悲剧但却辉煌的结尾——一场交通事故结束。一辆黄色的梅赛德斯无情地把她撞倒在地，然后逃离现场。然而，在玛卡贝娅自己看来，卡洛塔的预言却正在开始变成现实。躺在冰冷的地上，她看到的是存在于周围一切事物当中的希望。她感觉到自己在今天真的意识到了自己的存在，她重生了！她似乎变得越来越像个真正的玛卡贝娅，似乎真正到达了自己本身。她用剩下的力气慢慢地移动，摆出一副胎儿的姿势，这当然是她要重生的标志。她现在热情地渴盼死亡的拥抱。在渴望那甜蜜的虚无来临之时，她也拥抱了自我。在最后一口气、最后一点清醒意识离开她之前，她在脑子里不断地重复一句话：“我在，我在，我在。”(83) 此时，她对自我的意识已经使她有了前所未有的幸福感。

除此之外，死亡前的状态似乎与玛卡贝娅一直未得到的、某种强烈的感官渴望颇为相像。现在，她有了一种“与爱情一样令人愉悦、温柔、让人恐惧、让人心寒、但也同样具有穿透力的感受。”(83) 她将从“一个处女”(83) 变成一个真正的“女人”(83)，完成成人的仪式。现在，她完整了。

玛卡贝娅最后要说的话确实算得上是个胜利的宣言，非常激动人心。在那些仅仅把她看成是命运牺牲品的冷漠看客之前，她说：“至于明天。”(84) 曾几何时，这样的语言文字是她不得而入的禁区。现在，这文字却成了她的忠实奴仆，表达的是她的意思。说完这些话，她吐了一口血。那血就像是有着千道光芒的星星一般，突出着“每个人的伟大”(85)。

通过对两个迥然不同的人物的生动描写，利斯佩克托确实让读者接近了人生的神秘深处。不论是她对写作本身颇具独特性的解构，抑或是她独特的、今天读起来仍然同样震撼的女性写作风格，都让我们长久地驻足在她的写作疆域之中，流连忘返。

Chapter 13 Subversive "écriture Féminine" of Femininity and Writing Itself in Clarice Lispector's *The Hour of the Star* (Brazil)

For the famed French feminist literary critic Hélène Cixous, the Brazilian writer Clarice Lispector (1920—1977) is nothing short of being a great discovery, whose writings are believed to be the ultimate epitome of "écriture féminine", or "female writing". Arguably, Lispector does cut an all-too-striking figure with her trademark style that is hard to be imitated. It often subtly blends fiction and philosophy, and makes a creative interplay of narrator and character, never failing to surprise, move and inspire readers worldwide.

In *The Hour of the Star*, her consummate final novel, Lispector manages to create two utterly original characters—Rodrigo S. M., and Macabéa that bear all marks of her unique style. The former has double identities—both as narrator and character. From the beginning, this cosmopolitan figure is self-contradictory and unreliable in many senses. He constantly questions and doubts himself as a capable author (poor in describing things), and even asks himself why he writes about Macabéa and her story with its lack of depth. Therefore, his narration inevitably falls into a repeated pattern of interruptions and continuations. When his narration finally seems steady and logical, he claims to the readers that he is going to ensure his own impartiality and objectivity even at the cost of emotional barrenness. However, again and again, he tends to be easily emotionally involved. Throughout Macabéa's tale, he never stops giving his comments or showing his compositional process. He even constantly compares Macabéa's life with his own. He also claims to write a simple story, with its clear beginning, middle and end. However, his beginning is delayed infinitely, tiring readers with a terribly long preamble; the middle is rendered fragmentarily, constantly breaking off the narrative; the end is delayed, edited, rewritten time and again. When Macabéa is finally dead, he even feels himself to be also dead, indeed echoing Roland Barthes's "the death of the author".

The central character of the novel, Macabéa is an even more complex construct despite her deceptive simplicity. Arguably, this character is unprecedented in literary creation. She is from the slums of Northeast Brazil and born with a legacy of misfortunes: poor, stupid, dumb, ugly, and expressionless in her eyes, barely literate, anonymous, and invisible to others. Not only so, she is also not wanted, needed, or loved by anyone. Throughout her life, the best positions she can have in society are as an insignificant typist, and then as a metal worker.

What astonishes readers is her strange resilience amidst such obvious harshness. She is inwardly free, and has a rare, intuitive, and unconscious understanding of what real freedom means. In a largely unconscious manner, she seems to abide by her self-fashioned principle of "I am, therefore, I am."(36)① In her eyes, it is already wonderful enough to be alive. She is really quite happy, as purely so as an idiot, never being aware of her unhappy state.

---

① Clarice Lispector, *The Hour of the Star*, translated by Giovanni Pontiero (New York: New Directions, 1992). Subsequent citations to this work are given as parenthetical page references in the text.

She even wants to be a movie star like Marylyn Munro. Despite her nothingness, she has strong faith, not in a strictly religious sense, but nonetheless strong and dedicated. She always asks questions that are seemingly trivial or irrelevant to herself. She does not worry too much about her own future. Unlike her lover Olimpico and workmate Gloria, she has very vague class consciousness, never realizing the need to join the so-called privileged class and never realizing she is "a mere cog"(29) in the capitalist machine.

Even after being abandoned, betrayed and hurt by Olimpico, who ditches her for Gloria, she still feels no despair or hopelessness. In fact, she carries on her own life as if nothing had happened. Suddenly, an idea occurs to her—giving herself a treat now that no one is willing to love her. She even starts to paint her lips lavishly. In a way, this is the dawn of her female consciousness.

Ironically, the real turning point that achieves the transformation of Macabéa's life has something to do with one thing that has long denied her access—words. In her "climax of existence", her decisive encounter with Madame Carlota, she reaches a more conscious level of understanding what freedom truly means. This prostitute-turned-brothel boss-turned-fortune-teller first asks Macabéa to divide the cards with her left hand and then reads her destiny, exclaiming "what a terrible life you have!"(75) She goes on to say, "As for your immediate future, that's miserable as well. You're about to lose your job just as you've already lost your boyfriend"(75, 76).

However, after a while, she suddenly informs Macabéa of her good fortunes: she will become a new person, her boyfriend will return to her side for regretting his loss, her boss will change his mind about her job, and a foreign gentleman called Hans will suddenly bequeath his fortunes to her. This prediction suddenly induces in her an unprecedentedly fierce hunger and hope for the future. She feels that the range of possibilities for her is endless. Her hour has come. Ironically, in her excitement in finding the links between the present and the future, she finally recognizes that all along her life has indeed been miserable.

The nothing less than sensational narrative finds a tragic and yet strangely glorious end in a car accident: a yellow Mercedes mercilessly knocks her down before fleeing from the scene. However, in Macabéa's personal vision, Madame Carlota's prophecies are starting to come true. Lying on the cold ground, she nonetheless sees hope in everything around and feels this day, of all days, is the dawn of her existence: she is truly born. She seems to become more and more transformed into a Macabéa, as if arriving at herself. She has enough life left in her to stir gently and take up a foetal position, certainly a sign of the urge for rebirth. She is as eager as possible for the great embrace of death. While longing for that sweet nothingness, she embraces herself. While holding fast to the last breath and consciousness, she mentally repeats over and over again: "I am, I am, I am." (83) At this moment, the realization of herself fills her with unprecedented happiness.

What's more, pre-death seems to be like some intense sensual longing that has long been denied to Macabéa. Now, she has a sensation "as pleasurable, tender, horrifying, chilling and penetrating as love." (83) She is going to turn herself from "a virgin" (83) to "a woman" (83), consummating the ritual of adulthood. She is complete and whole now.

The final declaration on Macabéa's part is indeed nothing short of being victorious and breathtaking. Before the indifferent onlookers who treat her as a mere victim of chance, she utters this sentence composed of words that used to deny her access and now become

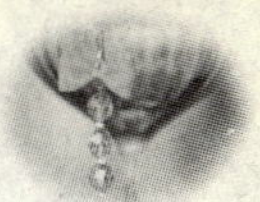

her slave: "As for the future."(84) Then, she vomits a little blood like a star with a thousand pointed rays, highlighting "the greatness of every human being"(85).

Through the vivid portrayal of two utterly different characters, Lispector does succeed in taking readers close to the mystery of life and leaves us deep in Lispector territory, with its unique deconstruction of writing itself, as well as its unique female writing style, a true marvel as astounding then and now.

第十四章　处女的历程

——读智利女作家露西亚·格拉的短篇小说《处女的激情》

当今许多拉丁美洲作家都有超凡的能力营造出普通人生、普通人魔幻、神秘的一面。这就是为什么读他们的作品经常意味着无限的惊奇、愉悦，还有难懂。在其中比较著名的女作家群中，智利的露西亚·格拉（1942—　）当然是个不错的代表。除了是个国际上知名的翻译家、取得了不错的学术成绩之外，她本人也是个能力很强的文体家，敢于探索人性深处所有真实、原始的情感。

在《处女的激情》中，格拉呈现了一个未婚女子对爱情深切的渴盼。从一开始，这个早已过了芳华岁月的女人就在写自己的故事，写她的沮丧与期待。她跟自己承诺，将来有一天，她一定要出去寻找她的白马王子，找到真正的自我。然而，承诺并不能保证什么。更糟的是，这些承诺甚至会让人产生错误的、根本不能够实现的希望，不断地折磨人，无法拯救。幸运（或者不幸）的是，她自己并不知道。

在这个家里，虽然她无法理直气壮地称它是自己的家，却必须要一直履行自己被设定的职责。她情不自禁地在别处寻找自己的“替身”，譬如电视里出现的、被流产的孩童，或者是描述老处女可怜生活的探戈歌曲。正是在这个时候，她突然想起了自己曾经的一段过往，看到自己“再次回到农家小屋的后院，再次回到很久很久以前的童年”(100)①。那时，她想从树上摘李子吃，但是

---

① 本章所引依据 *Short Stories by Latin American Women: The Magic and the Real*, edited by Celia Correas De Zapata (New York: The Modern Library, 2003). 引文后括号内的数字为引文在原著中的页码。

够不着。是园丁安士科来帮她的忙。他幽默的话语与关爱的语调给女孩带来了难言的温暖。二人躺在一起，说各种各样的笑话。在女人的记忆里，园丁成功地给她带来了“充满阳光、水果和温柔的慵懒之感。这种感觉经常在余下的夏日里反复出现”(101)。尤其有趣（或者说有些令人震惊）的是，园丁还有些不知羞耻地将自己的性器官暴露给女孩，跟她说这是个“真的很可爱的小动物，每次碰到漂亮的女孩子都会竖起来”(101)。应该注意到，安士科这里的行为绝不是为了表明他是个性变态。他只是以自嘲的方式（虽然有些另类）希望能够逗小女孩开心罢了。

与园丁安士科的这次改变人生的邂逅之后，处女的生活似乎一直在走下坡路。向她求婚的人来了又走，什么痕迹都没有留下。不幸的是，她必须把自己燃烧的激情深藏起来。不知道从哪天起，在她完全没有意识到的情况下，她就成了家里公认的老处女了。她必须要装作开心的样子来料理家务，来照顾家里其他人的孩子，就像是个女仆一样。似乎没人知道，或者愿意知道，其实这个老处女也有她自己想实现的承诺、想完成的梦想。

宛如命运安排一般，园丁安士科又一次来帮了她。在遗产分配典礼上，处女感到非常压抑。就在这时，她很偶然地看到了一张有安士科在正前方的照片。这张照片让她远离了眼前这一肃穆的情景，来到了那个只有她与安士科同在的世界。她情不自禁地说了一句话：“安士科，这么多年，很多事情都发生了，但是我一直没变。”(102) 换句话说，她仍然为他保守贞洁，只为了他一个人。这几乎让我们联想到加西亚·马尔克斯的《霍乱时期的爱情》了。

安士科神奇般的来临给处女的生活带来了新的希望和生机。所有那些让人疲惫不堪的家务活再也不算什么了。当她打盹的时候，她甚至能感受到安士科对自己颇具感官性的、温暖的抚摸，让她再次想起了“那个结满果实的夏天”(103)。她甚至感觉“安士科似乎有很多手指一般，指尖滑过她的每一寸肌肤”(103)。

处女的性幻想在自己的身体上留下了明显的印迹，但是似乎没有一个人知道它们真正的原因。此时，她的一个姐姐向她提了个建议，希望她去蒙特港度假散心。就这样，她出发了，借此也好逃离那些有关她单身生活的恶毒闲话，同时也可以给自己心爱的侄子阿尔伯托带去一份惊喜。而阿尔伯托也是唯一一个曾经与安士科见过面、并且知道他阿姨暗恋他这一事实的人。

在一次旅行过程中，处女的船停靠在了智鲁，并在那里知晓了一个被人称作是“巫师”(105)的人的存在。据一个老渔夫所说，这个叫作伊格纳西奥的人非常古怪，住在“山上的一座小屋里。而这屋子早就被附近的树林遮掩得严严实实”(105)。当处女终于到了小屋时，让她震惊不已的是，住在这里的这个男人不是别人，正是她亲爱的安士科，那个让她长久以来魂牵梦系、日思夜想的人。不仅如此，就像是谁施了魔法一般，这个安士科竟然“更年轻了，还留了小胡子”(105)。当他们终于面对面地交谈时，处女向他庄重、深情地表了白：“安士科，你真的不该不听我的话……我还是那个在无花果树下躺在你身边的纯洁女孩儿啊。”(105)对另一个人如此完全、如此绝对的专情，确实是震撼人心。再也没有任何事物可以阻碍他们了。说完这些有关爱情的豪言壮语，处女便开始了自己人生中最重要的仪式之一，那就是终于用自己的大腿把他庇护起来，“完成那个跳动的、饱含着血液与热蜡的仪式。”(105)

整个叙事中，处女即使面临的环境大多数情况下都是敌意的，但她却从未停止自己的渴望。她用想象力给自己编织了很多梦想和幻象，而且还展开了奇幻之旅，读来让人惊叹。女性成长的这一经久主题在拉美作家的这篇小杰作中再次得到了精彩的表达。

Chapter 14 A Virgin's Progress in Lucia Guerra's "The Virgin's Passion"(Chile)

Arguably, not a few of the Latin American writers have a rare ability to conjure the magical side in the ordinary life and people. This is why reading them often means infinite surprises, delights as well as difficulties. Among the noted women writers there, Chilean writer Lucia Guerra (1942—) is certainly a good representative. Along with her academic work as an internationally renowned translator, she herself is also a competent stylist who dares to explore all the true and primitive emotions hidden beneath the human skin.

In "The Virgin's Passion", Guerra presents an unmarried woman's deepest longings for love. From the beginning, this woman, already past her prime, is writing about herself, her frustrations and expectations. She makes a promise that one day she will seek her own true self on a quest for her prince charming. However, promises cannot guarantee anything. What's worse, they can even induce false and hopeless hopes that keep on tormenting people without salvation. Fortunately or unfortunately, she does not know it herself.

In the family which she cannot rightfully call her own and yet has to be dutiful all the time, the woman cannot help finding her "doubles" elsewhere, such as an aborted child on TV, or the Tango song that describes a spinster's miserable life. It is at this time she chances upon a precious old memory, seeing herself once "again in the back yard of the country house in that long-ago time of my childhood"(100)[①]. At that time, she wants to fetch a plum from a tree, but in vain. It is the gardener Antuco who comes to help her in this dreadful need. His witty words and loving tones bring a certain untold warmth to the girl. They lie down together, making all kinds of jokes. In the woman's memory, the gardener manages to lead her into "a lethargy of sun, fruit, and tenderness that recurred often throughout the rest of the summer"(101). Especially funny (or shocking) is the gardener's shameless exposure of his member to the girl, saying it is a "real nice little animal that rears up each time it sees a pretty girl"(101). It should be noticed that Antuco's behaviour here by no means shows he is a sexual predator. He just makes fun of himself and hopes to entertain the little girl.

After this life-changing encounter with the gardener, the virgin girl's life seems to go on a downward path. Her suitors come and go, leaving no trace behind. Sadly, her burning passion for love has to be shelved deep down. One day, even without her own knowing, she becomes the spinster of the family. She has to feign pleasure in taking care of the housing work, the children borne by her other family members, just like a maid. No one seems to know, or cares to know that this spinster also has her own promises and dreams to fulfil.

Once again, as if by fate, it is the gardener Antuco who comes to save her. In the legacy-distribution ceremony, the virgin girl feels very depressed, and chances upon a photo with Antuco in the

---

① *Short Stories by Latin American Women: The Magic and the Real*, edited by Celia Correas De Zapata (New York: The Modern Library, 2003). Subsequent citations to this work are given as parenthetical page references in the text.

foreground. This photo brings her away from the overly solemn scene into a world where only she and Antuco reside. She cannot help telling him a line that is almost reminiscent of Marquez's *Love in the Time of Cholera*: "Many things have happened during all these years, Antuco; but nothing has happened to me"(102). In other words, she still keeps her virginity for him, and him alone.

The magical arrival of Antuco fills the virgin's life with new hope and vigour. All the chores in the house that constantly burden her become nothing. When she dozes, she even feels the highly sensuous and warm caresses from him, reminding her again of "the ripe fruit of summer"(103). She even feels that "Antuco's fingertips seemed to multiply, roaming every inch of (her) skin"(103).

This fantasy on the virgin girl's part leaves visible traces on her body, yet no one seems to know the real cause. Following a suggestion given by one of the virgin's sisters, she sets off on a vacation to Puerto Montt, so as to escape the wicked gossips surrounding her unmarried life, and to give a surprise to her beloved nephew Albertito, the only one who used to meet Antuco, and knows about her aunt's secret passion for him.

In one of the journeys there, the virgin's boat docks in Chiloe, where she is informed of a figure who is compared to a "witch" (105). According to an old fisherman, this man, whose name is Ignacio, is very strange, living in "a hut already hidden among the trees on a nearly hill"(105). When the virgin finally finds the hut, to her utter amazement and shock, this man is no other than her beloved Antuco, who has haunted her dreams and imaginations for such a long time. Besides, as if by magic, this Antuco is "much younger, and wearing a moustache"(105). When they are finally able to talk face to face, the virgin makes a solemn and highly moving, electrifying confession— "You shouldn't have disobeyed me, Antuco… I am still the virgin girl who lay beside you under the fig tree"(105). This total and absolute devotion to a man is indeed all-breaking and overwhelming. Nothing can be in its way any more. With such heroic words, she finally goes through one of the most important rituals of her life, letting her thighs finally shelter him "in that pulsating ritual of blood and hot, spurting wax."(105)

Throughout the narrative, the unquenchable longings of the virgin in spite of the mostly hostile surroundings, as reflected by her self-fashioned dreams and fantasies, as well as her magical journey, is nothing short of breathtaking. The time-honoured motif of female bildungsroman again finds one of its most eloquent spokesman in this Latin American master's small masterpiece.

第四部分
当代大洋洲女性之声

Part Four
Contemporary Female Voices from Oceania

第十五章 作为性别战争场域的房屋

——读澳大利亚女作家斯尼亚·冈诺的短篇小说《母亲/家》

在当代澳大利亚文坛，女性作家异军突起，以她们明确的女权主义写作，吹来了清新、大胆、启人心智的新风，占据了中心的位置。在她们当中，斯尼亚·冈诺（1946— ）从各方面来说都是个杰出的代表。在她非传统的故事当中，她对主题和书写本身都做了大胆的新处理。

在《母亲/家》中，冈诺成功地让读者关注到了隐含于语言本身的权力和知识的互变性、流动性和不稳定性。正如小说具有高度实验性的英文标题“Mo（t）he（r）/H（t）ome（r）”暗示的那样，在父权意识形态之下，“家”与“母亲”基本上是同义。给“家（home)”加上两个字母，再换换字母的排列顺序，就变成了“母亲（mother)”；给“母亲（mother)”减去两个字母，再换换字母的排列顺序，就变成了“家（home)”。

对“家”之意义的争夺，就是整个故事的全部内容。在母亲看来，她的房子和身份都让她感到陌生，都不能充分、恰当地表达她真正的、已经被埋葬多年的自我。甚至在她做梦时（这个时间她应该能够完全由自己掌控)，她也从未梦到过她这个已经住了三十年的房子。

为了让她的房子真正变成“她自己”的房子，母亲设计了多个计划来对其进行大规模的整修，尤其是边上临时扩建的部分。然而，在父亲看来，房子“变化的过程”(8)① 不属于母亲的管辖

① 本章所引依据 *Frictions*：*An Anthology of Fiction by Women*，edited by Anna Gibbs and Alison Tilson（Melbourne：Sybylla Cooperative Press and publications LTD，1982）．引文后括号内的数字为引文在原著中的页码。

范围。母亲通过整修房子来满足自身需要，反映自我的心意已决，但是这个反映她“存在”(8) 的行为必须、只有以父亲“行为或者承诺行为”的方式才能得以完成。换句话说，女人没有权利亲自改变这个房子的样貌。她与整修房子联系在一起的自我只有在男人的控制之下才能得以实现。

经过近乎一辈子的不断谈判，他们最终达成了妥协——“让别处的别人”(8) 来帮他们选址、建房。不过，母亲仍然在一个方面坚持自己的想法，那就是要有一个“足够大的饭桌，能够让全家坐下，似乎这样就可以确保她们在陌生的土地上一代又一代繁衍生息，香火不断一样”(8，9)。当父亲死后，这个愿望终成泡影。父权形象的缺席使得室内战争也变得毫无意义。这一反讽似乎在表明当今激进女权主义的弊端，暗示着性别战争应该以理性、合理的方式进行，应该考虑各方的利益。否则，尽管追求女性主义的动机是好的，理想是远大的，结果却不一定能够真正令人满意。

Chapter 15 The House as a Site for Gender Wars in Sneja Gunew's "Mo (t) he (r) / H (t) ome (r)" (Australia)

In the contemporary Australian literary arena, a host of women writers take the central stage, bringing freshness, daring, and intelligence in their explicitly feminist writings. Among them, Sneja Gunew (1946—) is an outstanding representative in every possible way. In her unconventional stories, she takes liberties with both the subject and form of writing itself.

In "Mo (t) he (r) / H (t) ome (r)", Gunew manages to bring into sharp focus the interchangeableness, fluidity, and unstableness of power and knowledge inherent in language itself. As the highly experimental title implies, in patriarchal ideology, the "home" and "mother" are fundamentally the same thing. Adding two letters to "home", it becomes "mother"; subtracting two letters from "mother", it becomes "home".

This struggle for the meaning of "home" is exactly what the whole story is about. In the mother's eyes, her house and her body are both alien to her, hardly being able to fully and properly express her true self, which has been buried for years. Even in her dreams in which she is supposed to be capable of being on her own, she never dreams about this house that she has occupied for thirty years.

To make her house truly become "her" house, the mother sets up many plans to renovate it extensively, especially that corner mansion of makeshift extensions. However, in the father's view, the "becoming"(8)[①] of the mansion does not fall into the domain of a woman. Since the mother sets her mind on changing the house so as to satisfy her own need and reflect her self, this reflection of her "being"(8) can only be done through the father's "doing or promising to do"(8). In other words, the woman has no right to change anything about the house by herself. The self she associates with the renovation of the house can be fulfilled only when it is under the man's control.

Through constant negotiations that cost them almost a lifetime, they finally reach a compromise—having their future domestic productions sited and built "by others elsewhere"(8). But the mother still holds fast to one accessory— "the notion of a dining-table large enough to seat the whole expanded family, as though this would ensure our dynastic preservation, our survival on alien soil"(8, 9). This wish is finally made void due to the death of the father. The absence of the patriarchal figure renders the domestic warfare futile and meaningless. This ironically shows the underside of radical feminism nowadays, and implies that gender wars should be waged and conducted in a rational and reasonable way, taking into full consideration the interests of both sides. Otherwise, despite the high ambitions and good intentions in the feminist pursuit, the results may not turn out to be that satisfactory.

---

① *Frictions: An Anthology of Fiction by Women*, edited by Anna Gibbs and Alison Tilson (Melbourne: Sybylla Cooperative Press and publications LTD, 1982). Subsequent citations to this work are given as parenthetical page references in the text.

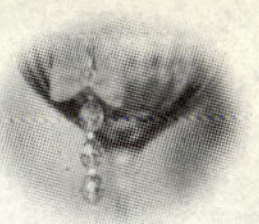

第十六章　处于疯狂边缘的女人

——读新西兰女作家珍妮特·弗雷姆的长篇小说《水中的脸》

在当代新西兰所有的女性小说家当中，似乎没有人可以与“神圣的”(艾丽斯·希伯德语）珍妮特·弗雷姆（1924—2004）相提并论。她的一系列获奖小说、诗歌都与她在精神病院里颇具创伤性，但也颇具启发性的经历紧密相关。

在弗雷姆的所有小说中，《水中的脸》可以说是医学话语最重的一本了。它在当代的语境下将福柯式的疯狂与文明进行了戏剧化的展示。

对于安妮塔·布鲁克纳来说，这本小说确实是“文学作品中对疯狂的最好记录……堪称杰作”。希拉里·曼特尔则认为“珍妮特·弗雷姆甚至比伍尔芙还自传化”。确实，从一个层面上来说，她的这本小说确实提供了一个有关疯癫的、很可信、很真实的病例记录，展示了那些专制的精神病院种种诱发恐慌与控制的非人机制。

对于主人公伊丝缇娜·玛维特（据珍妮特·弗雷姆本人说，这个人物的名是塞尔维亚－克罗地亚语，意思是真相；这个人物的姓是希伯来语，意思是死神）和其他病友来说，疯癫的第一个严重的后果便是“他们”与“我们”泾渭分明的划分。因为她们是病人，所以似乎就应该被整个世界“他者化”。她们被“正常”人隔离开来，甚至连她们自己的亲人都很少或者从来不探望她们。在精神病院里，一些医生与护士本来应该帮助她们康复，却也把她们看成是非人类，觉得她们不配被人尊敬或者关心——“人们似乎忘记了，他们同样也拥有值得珍视的人性，同样需要被关心、

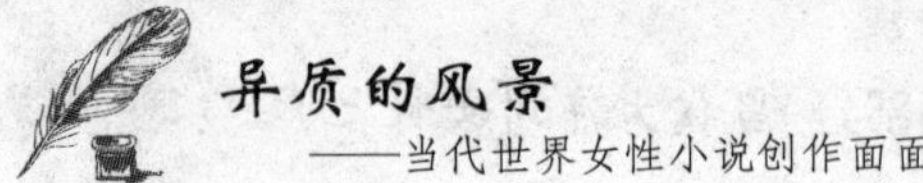

被爱"(96)[①]。甚至连病人自己都开始为自己现今的状况感到深深的羞耻，甚至怀疑、质问自身存在的意义。正如伊丝缇娜所说："我现在是已确定的（疯癫）公民了，我没有什么希望回去了……到处都是锁上了的门，还有用闩关上了的窗。"

面对这些精神病人的第二个严峻现实便是管理人员以非人性、羞辱人、令人恐惧的管理机制来控制、规训他们的日常生活。在这里，没人拿她们当成年人来看。相反，她们在很大程度上都被当做幼儿对待了。她们的每一个行为，甚至包括大小便，都被严格地、巨细无遗地甚至是施虐般地监管起来，没有被留给任何隐私的空间。不无讽刺的是，这些明显的、毫无羞耻的监视行为还往往披着关心病人的伪装。在这样的情形下，表现出一丁点不服从或者反叛行为的人都会被贴上"重病"的标签，转到其他"无希望"的病房去。甚至那些并没有明显表现出反叛性的人也被大大警戒，似乎他们如果表现出任何不安的样子，都是一种要被严厉惩罚的"犯罪"行为一般，活该遭受像前额脑白质切除手术这样洗脑的手术。事实上，恐惧无所不在，而且确实行之有效。譬如，在小说中，几乎所有的护士在看护病人时，都摆着一副让人畏惧的神情。譬如，似乎万能的格拉丝护士长，她宣称"我（伊丝缇娜）应该习惯医院的生活了，因为我已经在那儿待了很久了"(118)；哈妮护士，她养成了个习惯，那就是"在早餐时分突然说：'我今天要查你的寄物柜。'这个通知似乎充满着隐形的威胁，总是让人产生恐惧感，就好像在'查'我的寄物柜时，她可以偶然找到一些我忘记或者是没来得及藏起来的证物，最终把我定罪一般"(118)；布里琪护士，她看起来就像是个"女屠夫"(121)，和"那些颐指气使、麻木不仁的精神科护士几乎一模一样"(121)。那些很少来这里的医生也从来没有尽好保护、治愈这些病人的职

---

① 本章所引依据 Janet Frame, *Faces in the Water* (London: Virago Press, 2009). 引文后括号内的数字为引文在原著中的页码。

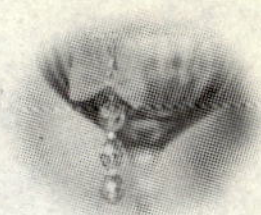

责，就像她们是护士们的私有财产一般。在他们看来，这些病人根本没救了，不如让其自生自灭罢了。

让疯人院情节变得复杂、使之变成“现实主义式”的小说（而不仅仅是记录）的主要原因在于珍妮特·弗雷姆使用的三个文学技巧，即伊丝缇娜矛盾的叙事视角、伊丝缇娜与护士布里琪之间模糊、让人摸不透看不清的关系，以及作者对病人们艺术性疯癫“表演”（而不仅仅是记述）令人兴奋、生动的描写。在很大程度上，伊丝缇娜与其他病人的双线虚构叙事把一个看似标准的案例文本变成了一个复杂、模糊、开放的文本，微妙地质疑、挑战、重构疯癫被固定化、模式化的定义。

首先来看伊丝缇娜的身份和认同感。她绝对不是个头脑简单的人。甚至在她所谓疯癫的顶点，她还是从未停止过对自身的思考，也未停止认真观察周围人以获得领悟。虽然她也有与其他病友看起来相似的恐惧和焦虑，但她的恐惧与焦虑其实已经与他们类似的情绪有很大的区别。当伊丝缇娜被有条件送出医院或干脆逃出医院时，这种区别便显得更加强烈。在这样的时刻，伊丝缇娜自己都觉得自己是个能够在边界两边出入的人了。疯狂还是不疯狂，变成了一个近乎偏执地困扰她的新问题。从情感上来讲，当与其他病友分开时，她觉得很孤独；她们在场或者在附近时，她才感到亲和力和归属感。然而，她也很期待被外面的那个大的世界所接受。精神病院内外的意识形态让她明白，在这里感受到归属感是没有希望、没有前途的。现在，在她观察自己之前的病友时，自己都情不自禁地采取了与那些护士、医生一样的立场。这种与所谓“正常”人认同的愿望并一定会得到他们的尊敬与认同是种讽刺，因为她从深层次上来说仍然是疯的，或者说是诗意般地疯（说好听点的话）。其实，它的意思就是，她与他们还是不同的。

如果说伊丝缇娜模糊的认同感已经成为一个未解的难题，那么她与布里琪护士之间令人迷惑的关系则以吊诡的方式提供了一部分的答案。正如小说着重强调的那样，这个令人畏惧的形象名字就很讽刺：她似乎应该是个将疯人与正常人联系在一起的“桥梁”。但是，事实上，她不仅不是“桥梁”，还成为兼监管、控制、威胁于一身的“文明”社会的一部分。她当然不会据尊降贵，和病人真心交朋友。然而，有趣的是，她这个本来应该威胁别人的人，却感觉被伊丝缇娜威胁。她甚至给她起了一个绰号“什么都知道的小姐”。很明显，布里琪护士对伊丝缇娜的恐惧难以理解。然而，细细思考，这种恐惧事实上反映了即使是那些所谓“心智健全”的人心中仍然存在的心理斗争。和伊丝缇娜一样，这些“心智健全”的人同样走在健全与疯癫的边缘。她们不能容许自己滑入疯癫的那一边。然而，与此同时，她们也无法永远保持理智。任何情感上的波动都会将她们颠倒。布里琪护士担心的不是伊丝缇娜这个人，而是她在她身上发现了与自己的相似之处——她们的身上同样都有模糊性，一方面希望远离疯癫，但是另一方面又不可避免地走向疯癫。

除了伊丝缇娜之外，其他精神病人也不像他们看起来那样被动或胆小。相反，很多病人都已经通过艺术方式找到了表达自身隐秘思想的途径。换句话说，他们已经找出或者设计出了自己独特的“疯癫语言”。这种语言高度个人化、主观化，充满着创造性的含义，只有有限的、同样具有创造性的听众才能够解码。这种语言不一定非要由书面文字组成。它可以是能够被掌控在手里、暂时性或者永久性地逃离权威的管束与控制的任何东西。譬如，米妮·克利夫的手绢，卡罗尔上面有“真微风”的“订婚戒指”，伊丝缇娜的故事书，希拉里寻找自己所爱之人的执着意志，还有布兰达的钢琴演奏，都让她们的声音成功地被他人听到，宣告了他们在这个世界上不争的存在。这种存在不会因任何手术或任何噩梦般的经历而被抹杀。

就这种创造性的“疯癫”艺术而言，珍妮特·弗雷姆确实有很多话要说。一开始，她便坦言说，这种艺术确实很难被大多数

无知或者不用心的外人所理解。在他们看来，这就只是一种无法被翻译的“外语”。相反，只有那些符合这些人心中刻板式印象的疯狂标志和姿势才会得到他们的关注。这时，他们就会像过分热情的“动物园学家”(143) 一样，纷纷以偷窥者般的目光来凝视这些“合理”(156) 疯狂的人群。

有趣的是，这种来自文明世界的简单、表面化、偷窥狂式的关注在伊丝缇娜这里遭到了最深刻的讽刺。她把他们与一个他叫做“格利菲斯先生”的老鼠作比。对于主人公来说，这只老鼠是“在砖建筑物、床垫棚子里住的老鼠，因此，它可是文明人呢”(182)。这种想当然认为的文明状态不难让读者联想到那些“动物园学家”的愚蠢。他们也许看起来心智健全，然而在理解像伊丝缇娜的这些精神病人方面，他们甚至连一只小老鼠都不如。

弗雷姆之所以要刻意强调这些“文明”人缺乏敏感度、愚蠢，无法弄懂精神病人的人性，绝不是仅仅为了自我指涉。相反，这使得小说又多了一层内涵，同时表露又掩藏了重要的信息。对于弗雷姆来说，这一隐藏的信息似乎是双向的。一方面，她确实希望文明世界可以对疯癫病人有更多的尊重与认同，能够更加敏感地面对这一边缘族群。另一方面，她也似乎在暗示疯狂也可以成为一个融入广大世界的很好策略。一个疯狂的艺术家可以通过表演疯狂或者参与疯狂仪式展现出艺术性疯狂的最大潜力。这么做并不是要满足那些偷窥狂的娱乐需要，而是为了证明另外一种人生的独特性、另一种美、另一种智慧和另一种风貌。它同样值得被公正对待。

小说的结尾并未给贯穿文本始终的问题与讨论提供一个简洁、无问题的终极答案，反而提出了又一个与疯狂相关的问题。在伊丝缇娜永久性地被保释出院时，一个护士给她提了一个建议：“你离开医院的时候，必须忘记你所看到的一切，把它们完完全全地从你脑海中抹去，就像什么都没发生过一样。然后，去外面的世界过正常的生活。”(223) 如果伊丝缇娜确实听了护士的建议，那么她就应该选择遗忘或失忆。然而，她却挑衅般地跟自己说："通过我写在这里的东西，你会看到我已经听了她的话，看到了没?"(223) 这种所谓的服从宣示确实非常讽刺，因为她事实上在这里记录了有关疯癫的一切。通过不忘记任何事情，伊丝缇娜经历了一场宛如受洗般的重生仪式。作为冥河式失忆的相反策略，这一效果看起来更加大胆、更加具有挑战性，从终极的意义上来讲也更具有深意。

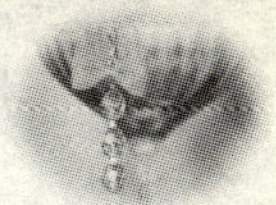

Chapter 16 Woman at Point Zero of Sanity in Janet Frame's *Faces in the Water* (New Zealand)

Among all the contemporary women novelists in New Zealand, none seems to equal the "divine" (Alice Sebold) Janet Frame (1924—2004), who has produced a large body of award-winning fiction and poetry that are closely and creatively related to her own traumatic and yet also enlightening experiences in mental hospitals.

In Frame's fiction, none other than *Faces in the Water* is more pervaded by a strong medical discourse that dramatises the Foucaultian understanding of madness and civilisation within the contemporary context.

For Anita Brookner, this novel is certainly "one of the most impressive accounts of madness to be found in literature … A masterpiece". For Hilary Mantel, " (e) ven more than Virginia Woolf, Janet Frame is the prisoner of her biography". Indeed, on one level, this novel does offer a highly convincing and highly realistic documentary case study of madness in authoritarian mental hospitals with their inhuman mechanisms of inducing terrors and controls.

The first serious consequence of madness for the protagonist named Istina Mavet (According to Janet Frame, the first name is Serbo-Croatian for truth, the family name is Hebrew for Death) and other mental patients is the clear-cut demarcation of "them" and "us". Due to their illness, they seem to be justifiably prone to the "othering" treatment from the rest of the world, suffering seclusion from the "normal" people, even their own families, who rarely or refuse to pay any visits to them. Within the mental hospitals, some doctors and nurses who are supposed to help them recover also treat them as non-human beings who deserve no proper respect or kindness from them— "It was forgotten that they possessed a prized humanity which needed care and love" (96)[①]. The patients even start to feel deeply ashamed of their own condition, doubting or questioning the meaning of their legitimate existence. As Istina says, "I was now an established citizen with little hope of returning. . . locked doors and barred windows."

The second grave reality facing the mental patients is the administrative staff's inhuman, humiliating fear-inducing mechanism of controlling and disciplining their everyday life. No one here is treated as a mature adult. Instead, they are largely infantilised, whose every act, even including pissing and shitting, is strictly, meticulously and even sadistically supervised, being left no room for privacy. Ironically, these overt and unashamed spying activities are often done in the guise of kindness for the patients. Those who show the least signs of disobedience or rebellion under such circumstances are labelled as severely ill, thus being transferred to other "hopeless" wards. Even those who do not show any overt sign of potential revolt are also greatly cautioned or warned, as if any sign of potential unrest on their side amounts to being a highly punitive "criminal" behaviour that deserves such a brain-killing, mind-destroying operation as leucotomy. In fact, fear pervades everywhere, and seems to be indeed working effectively. For

---

① Janet Frame, *Faces in the Water* (London: Virago Press, 2009). Subsequent citations to this work are given as parenthetical page references in the text.

instance, almost all the nurses here in the novel assume formidable looks when watching over the patients—the omnipotent Matron Glass, who claims that "I (Istina) ought to be used to life in hospital for I had been there long enough"(118); Sister Honey, who develops a habit of "saying suddenly at breakfast time, 'I'm going through your lockers today,' an announcement which seemed to contain a hidden threat and which always produced a feeling of panic, as if in 'going through' my locker Sister Honey would chance to find some evidence which I had forgotten or neglected to hide and which would finally incriminate me"(118); Sister Bridge, who looks like "a female butcher"(121), also "so much like that of other domineering, insensitive mental nurses"(121). The doctors who come rarely also fail to perform their duty in protecting and remedying these patients, as if they are the sole possessions of the nurses who are beyond salvation and should persist or perish by themselves.

What complicates the madhouse plot and makes it "realistically" fictional (not merely documentary) mainly lies in three literary devices employed by Janet Frame, namely the ambivalent fictional point of view from Istina, the ambiguous and confusing relationship between Istina and the nurse Sister Bridge, as well as the exhilarating and vivid portraiture of the "performance" (instead of mere account) of the patient characters' artistic madness. These two fictional narratives largely serve to shift an apparently standard case text into a complex and ambiguous open text that subtly questions, challenges and reformulates the fixed and stereotyped notion of what madness is and what it may mean otherwise.

To start with the identity and identification of Istina, she is never a simpleton. Even at the height of her so-called insanity, she never ceases to ask questions about herself, nor does she stop gaining insights from keen observations of people around her. Indeed, despite her enlightened minds, she is not free from fears and anxieties. However, these fears and anguishes on her part are already different from others', in spite of the apparent similarities they share. This difference is heightened when Istina is put on parole or escapes from the hospital. At that time, she finds herself to be someone who negotiates both sides of the boundary. To be mad or to be sane becomes the new question that constantly haunts her like obsession. Emotionally speaking, she feels lonely when apart from her fellow patients, and feels affinity and belongingness in their presence or vicinity. However, she is also eager to be accepted by the larger world. The ideology outside and inside the mental hospital drives home to her that to feel belongingness here is without hope or prospect. She herself cannot help adopting the same stance as the nurses and doctors when observing her former fellow patients, as if this can highlight her new difference. Ironically, this urge to identity with the so-called "normal" people does not necessarily earn her the respect and recognition from them, for she is still deeply mad, or poetically mad (put in a better way), that is, different.

If Istina's ambiguous identification already constitutes an unresolved issue, the confusing relationship between her and the nurse Sister Bridge paradoxically answers part of the question. As is highlighted in the novel, this formidable figure is ironically named as if she were a "bridge" connecting the sane and insane. As part of the supervising, controlling and menacing "civilised" community, she is certainly not to condescend herself by befriending her patients genuinely. However, she also feels threatened by Istina, who even earns an interesting nickname as "Miss Know-all" from her. Apparently, this strange fear on the part of Sister Bridge is hard to

understand. However, on second thoughts, this fear in fact mirrors the subtle negotiation going on even in the minds of so-called "sane" people. Like Istina, these "sane" people also tread on a precarious line between sanity and insanity. They cannot allow themselves to slip into the line of insanity. Yet at the same time they cannot always maintain reason. Any emotional turbulence may threat to turn them upside down. What Sister Bridge fears is not Istina per se, but the similarity she finds in her, the equal ambiguity in putting insanity at bay and yet inevitably being drawn to its side.

Besides Istina, the other patients are not as passive or timid as they seem to be. Instead, many a patient has already found out the ways to convey their forbidden thoughts by veiled artistic means. In other words, they have sought out or devised their unique "language of madness", which is highly personal, subjective, and loaded with creative meanings that are decipherable only to a limited and equally creative audience. This language is not necessarily made up of written words. It may be anything in their hands that temporarily or permanently get beyond the supervising control from the authorities. For instance, Minnie Cleave's handkerchief, Carol's "gagement ring" with its "real zephyr", Istina's story book, Hilary's single-mindedness in discovering the man she likes and in unashamedly having affairs with him, as well as Brenda's piano playing, all help to make their voices heard by others and assert their unmistakable presence in the world, which is not to be erased by operations or other nightmarish experiences.

Concerning this creative "mad" art, Janet Frame indeed has a lot to say. She starts by frankly acknowledging that this art is indeed hard to be understood by most ignorant or inattentive outsiders, who see this as a mere "foreign language" that is indecipherable. In contrast, only those signs and gestures of madness that conform to generalisations and stereotyping in popular minds get more than enough attention from the outside world, who, like zealous "zoologists" (143), rush to cast voyeuristic gazes on these "sensibly" (156) mad people.

Interestingly, this easy, superficial, and voyeuristic attention from the civilised world suffers one of the deepest ironies from Istina, who compares them with a mouse she calls "Mr. Griffiths". For the protagonist, this mouse is "a Brick Building and Mattress Shed mouse and therefore civilised" (182). This taken-for-granted civilised state never fails to remind the readers of the stupidity of those "zoologists". Those "zoologists" may seem to be sane, yet even a mouse can show more understandings of the mental patients like Istina.

This emphasis on the great insensitivity and stupidity of those "civilised" people, who fail to grasp the humanity of mental patients, is by no means self-referential. Instead, it adds a further shade of connotation that seems to be both revealing and concealing. For Frame, the hidden message seems to be bilateral. On the one hand, she does call upon greater respect and recognition from the civilised world, hoping for their greater sensitivities in face of the marginalised group. On the other hand, she also seems to imply that madness can serve as an eloquent strategy for fitting in the larger world. A mad artist can bring forth the best potential of artistic madness by both performing and participating in the ritual of madness. This is not to cater to the needs for entertainments of the voyeuristic people, but to argue for the uniqueness, the alternative beauty, wisdom and landscape of another kind of life and being that deserve a fair treatment.

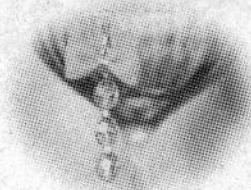

Rather than bring a neat and unproblematic closure to the questions and discussions that run through the text, the ending seems to pose another, although deeply related, question concerning madness. The advice given by one of the nurses to Istina on her permanent parole goes as follows: "When you leave hospital you must forget all you have ever seen, put it out of your mind completely as if it never happened, and go and live a normal life in the outside world."(223) If Istina does follow this nurse's advice, she is supposed to choose oblivion or loss of memory about everything that has happened in the mental hospital. Instead, she defiantly announces herself by saying "and by what I have written in the document you will see, won't you, that I have obeyed her?"(223) This announcement of so-called obedience is highly ironic in that she in fact keeps a record of everything about madness here. By forgetting nothing, Istina goes through a baptism-like ritual of rebirth. This effect, as a counter-move to Styx-like loss of memory, seems to be more daring, more challenging, and ultimately more deeply meaningful as a revelation.

第五部分
当代非洲女性之声

Part Five
Contemporary Female Voices from Africa

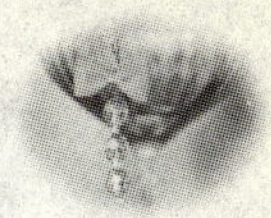

第十七章 动乱中意外的女性共鸣与和解

——读尼日利亚女作家奇玛曼达·恩戈齐·阿迪奇埃的短篇小说《私人体验》

在当今用英语创作的尼日利亚女作家当中，英国鞠子奖得主奇玛曼达·恩戈齐·阿迪奇埃（1977— ）总是能够牢牢地吸引读者的注意力。她的语言都经过精心锤炼，她讲故事的方法也颇有创造性，她探讨的主题也都很深刻，有关战争、种族民族纷争，还有这些外在事件对于普通人的影响。

在《私人体验》中，阿迪奇埃选择了一个看似最不可能的情景来前置故事当中的两个主人公：一家动乱中被废弃的商店。两个并不认识的女人，竟然不约而同地爬进了这家商店的窗户，目的只有一个，那就是逃避那些无法无天的暴民的伤害或者抢掠。颇为讽刺的是，这两个女人在各个方面都完全不同。奇卡是伊博人、基督徒，而且明显有较高的教育程度；而另外这个女人（叙事者并未提到她的名字）则是个有很重豪萨口音的北方人，几乎不怎么识字，还是个穆斯林教徒。考虑到这两种族裔、教派之前长久的纷争，她们最初对彼此都保持着警惕。

然而，这两个阴差阳错聚在一起的女人很快就消除了自己对对方的警惕。事实上，从故事一开始，奇卡就算是被穆斯林女人带路带到这里的。因此，在她的意识当中，这个穆斯林也许并不像伊博基督徒所说的那么暴力。

两个女人之间随后的对话确实证明了她们彼此之间可能会有的恐惧心理是没有根据的。很明显，穆斯林女人是反对自己教众在这场动乱中的暴力行为的，认为它是“邪恶之作”(50)①。毕竟，

① 本章所引依据 Chimamanda Ngozi Adichie, *The Thing Around Your Neck* (London: Fourth Estate, 2009)．引文后括号内的数字为引文在原著中的页码。

无辜的基督教徒被残忍地杀害了，而穆斯林平民的市场也被毁掉了。她从来没有让自己的信仰蒙住自己的双眼，她能清楚地看到现实。同样，奇卡在看到这个怀孕的穆斯林女人乳头受损之后，为了防止它进一步恶化，也给她提了很多使乳头湿润的建议。为了强化她们之间的联系，她甚至编了一个故事，说自己的母亲也生过五个孩子，就跟这个穆斯林女人一样。

当二人都为彼此的家人祈祷时，她们就更是加深了对彼此的理解、谅解。穆斯林女人庄重地向阿拉祈祷，希望他让奇卡的姐姐和哈莉玛都能身处平安之地。奇卡也向上帝祈祷，希望他能保佑穆斯林女人的女儿健健康康，不要因为这场突如其来的动乱受到任何伤害。这一肃穆或者是仪式性的时刻确实非常感人，因为它至少暂时性地移除了各种党派或者个人人为设置的那些高度限制性、非人性的界线。上帝与阿拉同样被人尊敬，同样被人祈求。有信仰的人都被理解、欣赏和尊敬着。不论是奇卡还是穆斯林女人都有她们自己的“私人体验”(52)。

当奇卡感到危险已经结束时，便坚持爬出了窗户。但她答应穆斯林女人，一定会回来接她出去。在回家的路上，她看到了很多躺在地上的尸体。有些尸体被烧得如此严重，她再也看不出他们到底是穆斯林还是基督徒了。这无异于是个及时而又无声的评论——所有人在死亡之时都没有什么区别。为了毫无意义的理由斗来斗去确实是件非常愚蠢的事情。

当奇卡履行自己的承诺，回来把穆斯林女人带出去的时候，穆斯林女人却惊讶地发现奇卡的腿上有血，便费尽心力帮她包扎伤口。甚至在离别时刻，这个女人还想着奇卡的利益，这让奇卡印象更加深刻。她终于知道了，温柔并不仅仅是专属于伊博基督徒的特性。豪萨的穆斯林人也能给人带来同样的温暖和柔情。在离别时，奇卡跟穆斯林女人要了头巾做礼物，来纪念她们在这场动乱中经历的一切。她们都对彼此祝福：“祝你的人民好！”(56) 应该注意到，在这个语境之下，用的是“人民”，而不是“家人”。

这似乎在暗示，和解的希望不仅仅发生在个人或者小团体之间，也可能发生在民族之间。

有关这次事件，BBC 广播把它报道成一个“宗教性事件，背后还隐含着族裔之间的紧张关系”(55)。对于奇卡这个已经大彻大悟的人来说，这样的报道再也不能让她信服了，因为在她身上发生的一切就这样“被包装、消毒，然后压缩成几个字”(55)。这样的报道连一半的事实都没有说到。事情远没有这样简单，人也不能仅仅被简化成只有单一的归属感。在暴力、不宽容与仇恨的大写“历史”之后，还有很多种个人的“历史”(譬如她与偶遇的穆斯林女人之间的历史)。这些“历史”都努力让自己不要陷入到吞没一切的大写“历史”当中，在最艰难的时世保持着最完整的人性，彼此交流、彼此帮助。事实上，BBC 片面的报道让奇卡如此生气，她甚至想把收音机扔到外面去。

《卫报》也同样对这个事件做了简化的处理，说“北部的、说豪萨语的穆斯林革命者一向有暴力反对非穆斯林的历史”(55)。在奇卡的眼中，这种高调的说辞也变得毫无道理，因为在她的私人体验中，她确实感受到了“一个既是豪萨，又是穆斯林女人的温柔”(55)。毕竟，信什么还是不信什么，个人的体验才是最有效的标准。

Chapter 17 Unexpected Female Affinities and Reconciliations in a Riot in Chimamanda Ngozi Adichie's "A Private Experience" (Nigeria)

Among all Nigerian women novelists working in English today, Orange-Prize winning author Chimamanda Ngozi Adichie (1977—) never ceases to seduce readers with her well-crafted language, her creative story-telling, and profound human themes touching upon war, racial and ethnic conflicts, and their impacts on ordinary lives.

In "A Private Experience", Adichie chooses a most unlikely setting to foreground the two main protagonists in the story: a deserted store in a riot. One by one, two women climb into the window of the store to escape being hurt or looted by runway rioters. Ironically, these two women are different in every possible way. Chika is Igbo and Christian, and obviously highly educated, while the woman (the narrator refrains from telling her name) is a Northerner with a strong Hausa accent, barely literate, and Muslim. Considering the long-time conflicts between these two racial and religious groups, they are initially quite alert to each other.

However, this alertness gradually loses its grip on these two women ironically linked together. In fact, from the very beginning of the story, Chika is somewhat led by this Muslim woman to this store for escape. Therefore, in her consciousness, she already feels that this woman may be not as violent in nature as Igbo Christians often accuse Muslims.

The following exchanges between these two women indeed

prove the groundlessness of the fear they may harbour towards each other. Obviously, the woman is against the violence committed by Muslims in this riot, saying it is "a work of evil"(50)①. After all, innocent Christian people are killed, and Muslim civilians' markets are also damaged. She never lets her faith blind her eyes to reality. On the other hand, Chika also gives the pregnant woman some good advice on moisturizing the nipples so as to prevent them from being damaged. To forge a bond between them, she even invents a story of her mother also having begotten five children, just like this woman.

A further understanding comes when they both pray for the safety of each other's family members. This Muslim woman solemnly prays to Allah to keep Chika's sister and Halima in safe places. Chika also prays to God to keep the woman' daughter safe and sound, free from the harm brought about by this unexpected riot. This solemn, even ritualistic moment is highly moving, for it removes the highly limiting and inhuman boundaries set up by various parties or individuals, at least temporarily. God and Allah are both respected and invoked. Those who believe in either of them are understood, appreciated and respected. Both Chika and the woman have their "private experience"(52).

When she feels the danger is over, Chika insists on climbing out of the window, promising to be back to fetch the woman out. On the way back home, she chances upon many bodies that lie on the ground. Some of them are burnt so seriously that she can never tell whether they are Muslims or Christians. This serves as a timely and

---

① Chimamanda Ngozi Adichie, *The Thing Around Your Neck* (London: Fourth Estate, 2009). Subsequent citations to this work are given as parenthetical page references in the text.

silent comment that all men are the same in death. To fight in life for such useless purposes is indeed foolish.

When she does honour her promise to take the Muslim woman out, that woman is shocked to find blood on Chika's leg. She takes pains to dress her wound with the containers she finds in the store. Even in their departing moment, she still thinks of Chika's interests. This further impresses Chika so much that she finally knows the gentleness is indeed not the sole property of Ingo Christians. A Hausa and Muslim can bring equal warmness and gentleness. Before their departure, Chika asks the Muslim woman her scarf as a gift, a memory for what they have both been through. They both say to each other: "greet your people" (56). It should be noticed that "people" instead of "family" is used in the context, implying the hope for reconciliation not simply between individuals or small units, but between peoples.

Concerning this incident, BBC radio reports as such: "religious with undertones of ethnic tension" (55). For Chika, the enlightened one, such reporting no longer convinces her, for everything is "packaged and sanitized and made to fit into so few words" (55), hardly covering half of the truth here. The matter is far from being so simple, the people cannot be reduced to a single belongingness. Behind the capitalized "History" of violence, intolerance and hatred, there are also many other kinds of "histories" or "her-stories", such as one between her and the Muslim woman in their accidental encounter, which try not to be involved into this all-submerging "History", keep the best of human nature intact, and communicate and help each other in the most difficult and trying times. In fact, the BBC's partial reports infuriate Chika so much that she even wants to throw the radio outside.

The newspaper *The Guardian* also makes a reductive reading of this incident by saying "the revolutionary Hausa-speaking Muslims in the North have a history of violence against non-Muslims"(55). This high-sounding claim also becomes groundless in Chika's eyes, for in her private experience, she does feel "the gentleness of a woman who is Hausa and Muslim"(55). After all, to believe or not to believe, personal experience is the most eloquent standard.

第十八章　创伤身体对“非此即彼”意识形态的质疑

——读津巴布韦女作家伊旺·维拉的《无名》

从很多意义上来说，获奖无数的津巴布韦作家伊旺·维拉（1964—2005）在非洲女性文学世界里都是个响当当的人物。她那高度诗化的语言，在很大程度上敢于碰触各种禁忌的暴力、颠覆性主题，确实暴露了这个饱经战乱的国家很多狰狞的现实。

在《无名》中，维拉将一个明显很敏感的时间——1977 年前置。这个时候，自由战争正在激烈地进行。殖民主义者仍然负隅顽抗，拼命坚守最后的阵地，还有他们在意识形态和文化上的影响。与此同时，信奉民族主义的游击队也同样要求津巴布韦人对他们完全地忠诚与服从。

在这样一个“非此即彼”、二元对立的语境之下，维拉通过塑造一个叫做马兹维塔的受害女性形象，问了一个非常严肃、也非常令人不安的问题。对于维拉来讲，任何来自外部力量的主叙事似乎同样具有压制性和滥用性，像她这样的女性都被排除在外。

具体来说，马兹维塔在面对殖民者时，当然对他们心怀仇恨，仇恨他们侵占自己的国土，仇恨他们迫使自己不断地流离失所，无家可归。然而，那些信奉民族主义的游击队对她也好不到哪里去。他们不仅复制了同样的霸权模式，将其用在被他们解放的国民身上，他们中的一些人甚至还对他们进行了严重的身体伤害。事实上，马兹维塔本人便是被一个管她叫“姐妹”的自由战士给强奸了。

马兹维塔的强奸事件具有高度的象征性意义，甚至其意义不仅仅限于象征。很明显，这是一个权力本身强加到无权之人身上

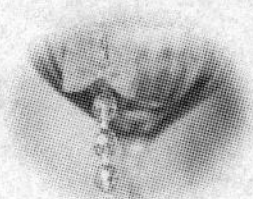

的显性标志，不论这权力来自何方（外国侵略者、国内的民族主义者，等等）。在一个更加深刻、可能有些讽刺的层面上，这一强奸事件也是马兹维塔自我意识的变态式觉醒，并随后展开对自我的追求（或复苏）。她开始感觉有些糊涂了，怀疑自己存在的作用和意义到底为何。她感觉自己没有名字了；自己的孩子同样也无名。

在随后的生活里，马兹维塔有过两位情人，先后是 Nyenyedzi 和乔尔。然而，随着马兹维塔与他们的交往，这种自我怀疑变得愈加强烈。尽管 Nyenyedzi 对她不幸的过去深表同情，但仍然觉得马兹维塔在成为好女人之前需要被他规训，因为她总是对祖国的含义缺少足够的感觉。换句话说，在他看来，她不够爱国。然而，这种典型化或者强迫性的民族主义让马兹维塔很难接受。再加上她之前还曾经被一个奉行民族主义思想的士兵那么严重地伤害过身心，就更无法接受这一思想。她真心觉得，殖民主义者与反殖民主义的战士在本质上和意图方面没有太大的区别。这种在观点上的根本分歧使得马兹维塔与 Nyenyedzi 终于分道扬镳，马兹维塔也踏上了去哈拉雷城的路程。

在哈拉雷，马兹维塔遇到了他生命中的第二个男人乔尔。他们开始过起了一种非常古怪的生活。没人告诉或者需要告诉对方有关他们过去的任何事情。他们只是"生活"在一起。对于他们来说，这无异于遵循完全自由的规定。然而，在乔尔得知马兹维塔怀孕之后，这种假装的、故意建构出来的自由很快就破碎了。乔尔并不想要这个孩子，因为他觉得这不是自己的亲生骨肉。尽管马兹维塔真挚地向他表白，乔尔还是不对这个受害的情人表现出丝毫的怜悯与同情，最后还无情地迫使她再次将自我流放。

两次被男人抛弃的马兹维塔情不自禁地意识到了一个真相，那就是各种形式的霸权在根本上都是具有同构型的，它们都会对少数族群或者少数个体残酷、非人性地加以边缘化。不论是殖民主义、民族主义，还是男性沙文主义，都剥夺了人固有的权益，都要求绝对、无条件的服从。在所有无权者当中，女性当然被划分在最低的阶层，被迫永远保持沉默，保持不在场的在场，隔离在宏大的主叙事之外。

这种灰暗但却真实的人生观让马兹维塔急于排解自己压抑已久的情感，她做了一件让人难以想象的事情——杀婴。这一行为使她几乎丧失了心智——她不断地说自己已经“把孩子的脖子弄断了”(109)[①]。

从某种意义上来说，杀婴这一可怕的行为之所以会发生，不仅是因为马兹维塔对自己人生和未来的狭隘视角（她想通过这一行为改变自己孩子和自己无名的命运），也是因为集体压迫性力量的运作。

当马兹维塔回到她出生的地方——Mubaira 时，她的拯救终于来临。在那里，她的母亲饱含深情地叫着她的名字，她也想起了这里的各种声音，打算把它们传承下去。只有在这时，她才“弯下腰去，把孩子从背上放了下来，放到自己的怀里”(116)。从“背上”到“怀里”，这个孩子（这里当然是个想象的存在）经历了一个象征性的仪式——从一个具有压迫性的创伤重负，变成了一个充满爱的、充满未来希望的重生之物。

---

① 本章所引依据 Yvonne Vera，*Without a Name* and *Under the Tongue*（New York：Farrar，Straus and Giroux，2002）. 引文后括号内的数字为引文在原著中的页码。

Chapter 18 Interrogating the "Either/or" Ideology on the Traumatic Body in Yvonne Vera's *Without a Name* (Zimbabwe)

In more than one sense, award-winning Zimbabwean novelist Yvonne Vera (1964—2005) emerges as a very striking presence in African women's literary world. The highly poetic language and largely violent, subversive themes that often dare to touch upon various taboos indeed reveal much of the unpleasant and grim reality in this war-torn country.

In *Without a Name*, Vera foregrounds a markedly sensitive time—1977, a time when the liberation war was raging in its most fierce manner. Colonists still desperately tried to retain their last stronghold, as well as their ideological and cultural influences. At the same time, nationalistic guerrilla also claimed equal, undivided loyalty and obedience from the Zimbabweans.

In the context of this "either/or" binary oppositions, Vera poses a very serious and unsettling question by portraying a victimized woman figure named Mazvita. For her, the master narratives by any outside forces seem to be equally oppressive and abusive, to the exclusion of women like her.

Specifically speaking, faced with the colonists, she certainly harbours strong hatred for their dispossession of her homeland, forcing her to go on endless exiles from place to place. However, the nationalistic guerrilla treats her no better. Not only do they reproduce the same hegemonic pattern and apply it those citizens liberated by

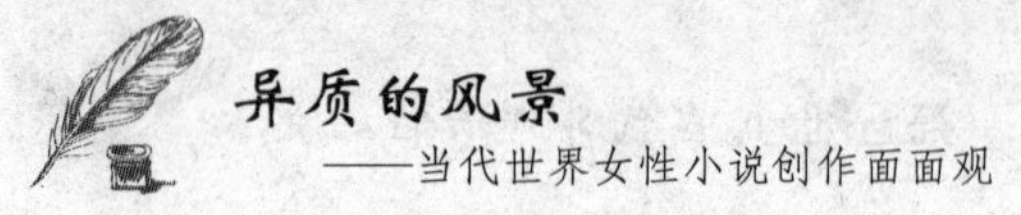

them, some of them even perpetrate severe bodily harms on them. In fact, Mazvita herself is violently raped by none other than a liberation soldier who even calls her "sister".

The rape of Mazvita is highly symbolic and much more. Certainly, it is a strikingly present sign of victimization imposed by power itself on the powerless, no matter where it comes from (foreign invaders, domestic nationalists, etc). On a more profound and possibly ironic level, this raping incident is also a perverted awakening of Mazvita's awareness of individuality and the ensuing quest for self-discovery (or recovery). She starts to feel confused, doubting the role and meaning of her existence. She feels herself to be without a name; her child is equally nameless.

This doubt is heightened during her respective stays with her lovers, namely Nyenyedzi and Joel. Despite the former's sympathy for her tragic past, he still feels that Mazvita needs disciplining before being a good woman, for she falls short of having a sufficient sense of the meaning of the homeland. In other words, she does not love her country and land enough. This version of archetypal or compulsory nationalism repulses Mazvita, especially concerning the fact that she herself is severely hurt and damaged by a nationalistic soldier. She really finds it more and more difficult to differentiate the colonists and the anti-colonial fighters in their basic nature and sinister intentions behind their respective acts. This fundamental departure in view finally destroys their relationship, setting Mazvita on the journey to the city Harare.

In Harare, Mazvita encounters her second lover Joel. They begin to lead a very strange life. No one tells or needs to tell each other anything about their past. They simply "live" together. For them, this amounts to following the rule of absolute freedom.

However, this feigned and deliberately fashioned freedom is quickly shattered by Joel's knowledge of Mazvita's pregnancy. For him, this child is not wanted, for he is not his biological child. Despite Mazvita's sincere confessions, Joel fails to show any sympathy for this victimized lover, relentlessly driving her way onto another exile.

Twice abandoned, Mazvita cannot help feeling much aware of one truth—the concurrence and fundamental homogeneousness of oppressive hegemony and power in all forms, as well as their cruel and inhuman marginalization of the minority groups or individuals. Colonialism, nationalism, male chauvinism—all these three dispossess one of his endowed rights and interests, and demand absolute, unconditional obedience. Among the powerless, women are certainly already fixed in the lowest rung, being forced to keep an eternally silent, absent presence, excluded from the grand master narratives.

This terribly bleak and yet ultimately true view of life leads Mazvita to commit an unthinkable act for desperate release of her long repressed emotions—infanticide. This act renders her almost out of her mind—she keeps on saying that she has "broken the neck of her child" (109)①.

In a sense, this appalling occurrence of child-killing is attributed not only to Mazvita's equally narrow perspective on her life and future (she wants to change the nameless fate of her child and herself with this act), but also to the collective oppressive forces at work.

The redemption finally comes only when Mazvita returns to the place of her beginning—Mubaira where she is lovingly called her

---

① Yvonne Vera, *Without a Name* and *Under the Tongue* (New York: Farrar, Straus and Giroux, 2002). Subsequent citations to this work are given as parenthetical page references in the text.

name "Mazvita" by her mother, remembers the various voices from this place, and intends to carry them on. Only then she "bends forward and releases the baby from her back, into her arms"(116). From "back" to "arms", the baby undergoes its ritual of symbolical transformation from an oppressive burden of trauma to a loving rebirth of hope for the future.

参考文献

[1] AJAY HEBLE. The Tumble of Reason: Alice Munro′s Discourse of Absence [M]. University of Toronto Press, 1994.

[2] ALICE MUNRO. Something I' ve Been Meaning to Tell You [M]. Vintage Books, 2004.

[3] AMY KAMINSKY. Reading the Body Politic: Feminist Criticism and Latin American Women Writers [M]. University of Minnesota Press, 1992.

[4] ANITA BROOKER. A Friend from England [M]. Vintage Books, 2005.

[5] ANNA GIBBS, Alison Tilson. Frictions: An Anthology of Fiction by Women [M]. Sybylla Cooperative Press and Publications LTD., 1982.

[6] BRENDA COOPER. To Lay These Secrets Open: Evaluating African Literature [M]. David Philip, 1992.

[7] CELIA CORREAS DE ZAPATA. Short Stories by Latin American Women: The Magic and the Real [C]. The Modern Library, 2003.

[8] CHERY ALEXANDER MALCOLM. Understanding Anita Brookner [M]. University of South Carolina, 2002.

[9] CHIMAMANDA NGOZI ADICHIE. The Thing Around Your Neck [M]. Fourth Estate, 2009.

[10] CLAIRE CASTILLON. My Mother Never Dies [M]. Translated by Alison Anderson. Houghton Mifflin Harcourt, 2009.

[11] CLARICE LISPECTOR. The Hour of the Star [M]. Translated by

Giovanni Pontiero. New Directions, 1992.

[12] DOUGLAS N. SLAYMAKER. The Body in Postwar Japanese Fiction [M]. Routledge Curzon, 2004.

[13] EFRAIM SICHER. The Return of the Past: The Intergenerational Transmission of Holocaust Memory in Israeli Fiction [J]. An Interdisciplinary Journal of Jewish Studies 19: 2 (Winter 2001): 26-52.

[14] GAY WILENTZ. Binding Cultures: Black Women Writers in Africa and the Diaspora [M]. Indiana University Press, 1992.

[15] GEORGE SOULE. Four British Women Novelists: Anita Brookner, Margaret Drabble, Iris Murdoch, Barbara Pym: An Annotated and Critical Secondary Bibliography [M]. Scarecrow Press, 1998.

[16] JAMES CARSCALLEN. The Other Country: Patterns in the Writing of Alice Munro [M]. ECW Press, 1993.

[17] JAN CRONIN, SIMONE DRICHEL. Frameworks: Contemporary Criticism on Janet Frame [M]. Rodopi, 2009.

[18] JANE GALLOP. Thinking through the Body [M]. Columbia University Press, 1988.

[19] JANET FRAME. Faces in the Water [M]. Virago Press, 2009.

[20] KATE MCMILLAN, ELIZABETH MCLEAY. Rethinking Politics: New Zealand and Comparative Perspectives [C]. University of Minnesota Press, 1992.

[21] LE MINH KHUE. The Stars, The Earth, The River [M]. Translated by Bac Hoai Tran and Dana Sachs. Curbstone Press, 1997.

[22] LI YIYUN. A Thousand Years of Good Prayers [M]. Random House, 2005. Linda Anderson. Plotting Change: Contemporary Women' s Fiction [C]. Edward Arnold, 1990.

[23] LUCIE ARMITT. Contemporary Women' s Fiction and the Fantastic [M]. Macmillan, 2000.

[24] LUDMILA ULITSKAYA. Sonechka: A Novella and Stories [M]. Translated by Arch Tait. Schocken Books, 2005.

[25] MARGARET ATWOOD. Negotiating with the Dead [M]. Cambridge University Press, 2002.

[26] MARIA ORNELLA MAROTTI, GABRIELLA BROOKE. Gendering Italian Fiction: Feminist Revisions of Italian History [M]. Fairleigh Dickinson University Press, 1999.

[27] MARK A. HEBERLE. A Trauma Artist: Tim O´Brien and the Fiction of Vietnam [M]. University of Iowa Press, 2001.

[28] MARTHA KING. New Italian Women: A Collection of Short Fiction [C]. Italica Press, 1989.

[29] MERJA MAKINEN. Feminist Popular Fiction [M]. Palgrave, 2001.

[30] MICHÈLE ROBERTS. Food, Sex and God: On Inspiration and Writing [M]. Virago, 1998.

[31] NOBUCO TAKAGI. Translucent Tree [M]. Translated by Deborah Iwabuchi. Vertical, 2008.

[32] ODILE CAZENAVE. Rebellious Women: The New Generation of Female African Novelists [M]. Lynne Rienner Publishers, 2000.

[33] PATRICIA DUNCKER. Sisters and Strangers: An Introduction to Contemporary Feminist Fiction [M]. Blackwell, 1992.

[34] PAULINE KALDAS, KHALED MATTAWA . Dinarzad' s Children: An Anthology of Contemporary Arab American Fiction [C]. University of Arkansas Press, 2009.

[35] PHIL POWRIE, MARGARET ATACK. Contemporary French Fiction by Women: Feminist Perspectives [C]. Manchester University Press, 1991.

[36] RINO ZHUWARARA. An Introduction to Zimbabwean Literature in English [M]. College Press, 2001.

[37] ROBERT MUPONDE, MANDI TARUVINGA. Sign and Taboo:

Perspectives on the Poetic Fiction of Yvonne Vera [M]. Weaver Press, 2002.

[38] ROBERTA RUBENSTEIN. Home Matters: Longing and Belonging, Nostalgia and Mourning in Women's Fiction [M]. Palgrave, 2001.

[39] SAVYON LIEBRECHT. Apples from the Desert: Selected Stories [M]. Translated by Marganit Weinberger-Rotman, Jeffrey M. Green, Barbara Harshav, Gilead Morahg, et al. The Feminist Press, 1998.

[40] SLAVENKA DRAKULIĆ. The Taste of a Man [M]. Translated by Christina Pribichevich Zoric. Abacus, 1997.

[41] STEVEN SALAITA. Modern Arab American Fiction: A Reader's Guide [M]. Syracuse University Press, 2011.

[42] Susan Minot. Lust and Other Stories [M]. Vintage Books, 2000.

[43] SUSANNAH RADSTONE. Sweet Dreams: Sexuality and Popular Fiction [C]. Lawrence and Wishart, 1988.

[44] TATIANA V. Keeling Surviving in post-Soviet Russia: Magical realism in the works of Viktor Pelevin, Ludmila Petrushevskaya, and Ludmila Ulitskaya. ProQuest [M]. UMI Dissertation Publishing, 2011.

[45] YVONNE VERA. Without a Name and Under the Tongue [M]. Farrar, Straus and Giroux, 2002.